Dangerous Course

A Douglas Lake Mystery

Eric M. Howe

Dear Reader -

Dangerous Course is the third book involving Erasmus Parsons, Heather Wilkins, and the Biological Station on Douglas Lake.

I hope you enjoy the story. If so, please recommend it. It is available on Amazon in both hard copy and Kindle versions – though I am certainly happy to send an electronic version free to anyone who wishes.

Please forgive any missed typos – I've tried to be thorough in editing, but undoubtedly something will slip through. This isn't my "day job" but rather a hobby.

If you have feedback or suggestions ... please reach out. I take constructive criticism well ☺.

Kindly,

Eric

emhowe@assumption.edu

Books:
- A Paxton Year
- Cycle of the Seasons
- Illumination: The Newton Secret
- Entanglement: The Newton Secret, Book 2
- Deadly Restoration: A Douglas Lake Mystery
- Gathering Moss: A Douglas Lake Mystery
- Dangerous Course: A Douglas Lake Mystery
- Douglas Lake Essays

Front cover image: Taken by the author, circa 1982.

FORWARD

Though this is a work of fiction, it is based on locations in and around the area of Douglas Lake in Northern Michigan. Of course, while the characters are imaginary, I've taken bits and pieces of so many wonderful friends and acquaintances to assemble the story.

There was at one time a fairly robust fleet of Lightning sailboats on the lake, and I was fortunate during the formative years of my life to be included as a crewmember for several different skippers. Those were golden summers in many ways, and I am sorry thesᵉ beautiful boats and so many of the wonderful peoᵒ who loved sailing them, have gone into twilight.

Sometimes now, when I am with frienᵈ are doing some sort of strenuous exercise, I shouting, "Hike for those turkey dinners!ᵗ bewildered looks. How can I explain thᵇ to them - the way we felt as boyˢ bellowed these same words to us ᵖ dangerously to windward from the lake?

Please forgive the liᵗ description of campus lifᵉ Michigan Biological Statioᵗ grossly oversimplified thᵉ represented that wonderᵗ

A northwest wind blows down the length, creating waves that begin as mere disturbances near Maple Bay, where cottages lay protected in the lee of the offshore tempest rushing through the trees overhead. Farther out, where the deep water begins, small furls take shape, each hinting at the possibility of forming bubbles of curling water near their summits. They rise and travel, attempt to show something of maturity, and vanish just a quickly as they descend onward toward the fishtail horizon so far away.

The wind keeps encouraging, past the tip of the island as it pushes the waves higher yet, and where before was the hint of something turbulent within the darker blue, now each summit falls upon itself as brilliant white splashes and spray - the whitecaps begun. They form and cascade and disintegrate, caught in the pull of the driving wind.

Further on they reach the neck between Grapevine point to the south and Sedge point to the north. Some discard themselves along the shore on either side, their wave action spent upon the sandy beach. Most pass through, gathering strength until they come before the eastern land, where the Big Shoal stretches beneath the lake – an underwater sandbar from one Fishtail to the other, reaching outward to meet the coming assault.

The waves make a transition from the deep water of the inlet bay to the shallows of the shoal and quickly lose their volume and power, spending their energy upon the sandy bottom, which is pulled slowly outward with each passing front. The shoal evolves in response - the sand bar beneath growing and shifting as one season turns into the next.

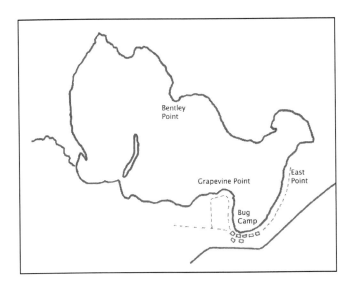

Bentley
Point

Grapevine Point

East
Point

Bug
Camp

Lake
Michigan

Mackinaw
City

Douglas
Lake

Good Hart

Harbor
Springs

Little Traverse Bay

Chapter 1

Thirty years ago.

The wind had been building since daybreak, beginning initially as small ripples on what remained of the glassy water from last evening's calm. It passed through the deep greens of the tree line along the western shore, where a golden sunrise first made its appearance on cottages tucked within reaching pines. By midmorning, it had gathered strength as the land continued to warm and pushed eagerly across the lake's surface, creating small waves that sought the opposing shore. These formed small curls upon their crests and reflected back a dozen shades of deep water blue, broken in places where they spilled upon themselves as frothy white caps in small cascades for a dozen yards or so until they petered out.

Tom waited until the *Deliverance's* bow broke the invisible line connecting the starting buoy off the port side with the anchor line of the old pontoon committee boat fifty yards away to starboard. He then turned the boat abruptly into the oncoming wind, causing the sails to suddenly lose their shape and began flapping noisily, each pulling haphazardly on their trim lines, making them bang this way and that against the foredeck and the main blocks.

A teenager with tousled brown hair leaned in toward the front of the cockpit and squinted at the gimbaled compass set several inches before the mast. "It's shifted around five degrees to north at two-seven-five," Jack said over his shoulder, waiting a few seconds more to check once again as the compass lolled back and forth in the oncoming chop. "Yep. Still two-seven-five."

The older man's eyes continued to scan ahead as he kept the boat pointed toward the windward coast. "If this shift holds, I don't want to come into the windward mark like last race, especially if the Horizon repeats." He glanced quickly at the wagging boom end nearest his spot in the aft, noting how it wavered to the left side. "The pin end of the line is favored," he said and turned his attention to the boy seated up front. "Ready on the watch?"

Another boy lowered himself cautiously off the gunwale onto the cramped fiberglass bench. He bent low and peered out across the starboard side toward the committee boat, almost hitting his head against the sway of the boom as it moved in tandem with the flapping mainsail. Rick nodded absently as he continued to stare toward the pontoon boat, his eyes quickly finding his left wrist to make sure the count down timer was reset. "I think she's getting ready."

Tom gently eased the tiller toward him and reached up to push the boom to windward, causing the mainsail to fill slightly as the boat went slowly backward and curved until it was once again on a starboard tack. "Keep an eye on her. I'm going to take us around the pin and come up under the field."

The boys scrambled across the centerboard trunk to their opposing stations as the sails filled. Jack lifted the main sheet from the ratchet cleat and played out several feet of line as Tom allowed the boat to fall off to leeward in a sloping arch around the mark. Rick clenched the jib line in his left hand and placed his right thumb on the main button of his watch, flinching slightly when he caught sight of the orange start buoy passing within a foot of their hull, held in place by a faded white rope that disappeared beneath the waves in a ghostly line toward the unseen bottom.

"You've got the *Serendipity* coming up at eleven o'clock," Jack said evenly, busying with preparations to jibe while the boat continued its gentle curve downwind.

Tom finally seated himself as they neared a dead run, pushing the tiller a little to starboard to adjust course and seeing a light blue hull with red pin striping come into view and pass within ten feet of their port beam. Rick looked quickly at the teenagers who crewed, laughing softly when a blonde haired girl in the fore position stuck her tongue out at him and then grinned foolishly. "So it's double or nothing then?" shouted the opposing skipper with a teasing expression as their hull dipped suddenly into the trough of a large wave that ran between them. A plume of spray shot up from the bow as they passed, splashing Rick as the Serendipity's stern

—
9

cleared their mast.

Tom considered giving a sarcastic reply but was interrupted by a pitiful lilting tone coming from the direction of the start line upwind.

Rick quickly pushed the start button. "I got it," he yelled, glancing to port across the water toward the committee boat. On the platform bow stood a stout older woman in khaki shorts and a large white t-shirt, holding a bullhorn in her outstretched arm toward the direction of the half dozen clustered sailboats nearby. A moment later, Rick saw her put the horn to her lips.

A tinny voice came crackling across the water, mixed with the white noise of the wind through the rigging as Tom arched the boat into a jibe. "That's five minutes!"

"Ready to jibe," Tom stated evenly.

Both boys ducked instinctively and began to step carefully across the centerboard as the wind caught the mainsail's leeward side and accelerated it violently across the cockpit.

A boat with a salmon-colored hull trailed loosely behind them by a hundred yards and executed the same course change, delaying its jibe enough to emerge downwind several boat lengths behind. An older man held the tiller and nodded pleasantly in their direction.

Tom looked over and yelled playfully. "Stop following me, Maury."

The man reached over the gunwale and padded the faded hull. "We need all the help we can get. Not fair this wood hull against you fiberglass boys. How's about luffing ten seconds at the start line?"

Tom snorted and shook his head slightly, pushing the tiller to starboard to bring the bow closer to the wind. "Let's tighten up a little," he said to both boys. "We'll reach across for a few minutes before tacking back and going under the field toward the pin." He looked quickly to windward, reading the various patches of rippled water where the breeze showed itself in darker shades.

The salmon boat tacked suddenly. "At least you could do a three sixty at the start!" pleaded the elderly man while he waited for his crew to adjust the sails for their new heading.

Tom laughed this time but said nothing further, instead studying the remaining four boats which began to assemble themselves in anticipation below the line. His eyes narrowed. "Where's the *Horizon*?"

Jack pointed to starboard a little downwind from their position. "They're below us still headed toward Ingleside." His eyes met Rick's. "I bet you he tacks over at the one minute and runs down the line."

Rick swiveled his head toward the start line, watching as the other boats began to jockey in loose formation closer to the pin end. He then checked his watch and looked back toward the white hull of the *Horizon* still headed away from the field. "He just tacked over!" Rick said.

"Then let's go," Tom replied quickly. "Ready about! Jack, let the sheet ease as we come over so the main luffs. Rick, I want to reach across using just the jib, so get it set."

Rick used his free left hand to grab the slack jib sheet that dangled loosely from the block as he prepared to step once again across the centerboard. When the boat began to tack over, he felt the windward side dip slightly and the bow start to arc its way to the left against the far tree line. In one motion, he crouched and crab walked cautiously to the right, jerking upward with his hand to release the leeward jib line held fast in the cleat while pulling simultaneously with his other on the loose line to help draw the sail across the foredeck.

Jack eased the main sheet as the boat came across, slowing their turn and reducing their forward speed on the new heading. Tom's attention remained on the cluster of boats closer to the pin end a couple hundred yards ahead. "Time?" he said curtly.

Rick fiddled with the jib adjustment and had just enough to peek at his watch. "Almost a –" The bullhorn sounded in the distance. "Minute," he trailed.

Tom looked quickly behind them. The *Horizon* was rapidly closing with her sails trimmed. "Jack, start bringing in the main slowly. I want some boat speed when he makes a move."

"Forty five seconds." Rick said evenly.

Jack slowly hauled in the sheet, drawing the line through the cleat while he watched the sail overhead take shape and felt the boat began to heel.

Rick saw the white hull veer suddenly from their wake as its crew trimmed the sails, lifting it windward on a close course toward the committee boat. "He's going above us!" he said excitedly, glancing again quickly at his watch. "Thirty seconds."

Jack's eyes caught a flicker of motion to leeward through the sail's clear panel above the boom. "You've got the Osgood boat coming below us on port."

"How soon?" Tom barked then added immediately before Jack had time to answer. "Are we clear?" The *Deliverance* now moved quickly in a reach fifty yards below the approaching start.

"Not if we go for the pin!" Jack said insistently.

Rick knew the timing was critical. The *Deliverance* could hold its course and duck below the oncoming dark blue hull of the Osgood boat before adjusting windward in a beat toward the pin end. However, it was certain the blue boat would tack to cover and gain an advantage by staying above them. Tom shot another glance toward the *Horizon*, judging his rival had decided for clear air nearer the committee boat. "Let's go then!" he boomed. "Sheet in both of you, and let's get her flat."

Both boys pulled quickly on their lines, bringing the sails close to the boat's midline as they maneuvered themselves carefully up and onto the heeling gunwale. Tom pushed the tiller further to leeward to bring the *Deliverance* on a close haul to the start. Waves clapped in rapport against the boat's yellow hull, and Rick's legs strained against the hiking strap as he thrust his upper body outward across the water.

"Starboard!" Tom shouted in the direction of the approaching blue hull.

"Ten seconds," barked Rick.

The Osgood boat considered tacking over immediately to avoid the right-of-way penalty but decided in a split second to bear off below the *Deliverance's* stern.

The boys eyed them momentarily as they passed only a couple feet to stern.

"Three, two, one," Rick counted calmly, followed by the lilting horn from the pontoon boat.

The *Deliverance* crossed the line two thirds of the way toward the pin, with three other boats beneath them. Jack looked quickly over his shoulder. "The *Horizon* cleared near the Committee Boat and just tacked over onto port. Osgood's staying on course just below him. I can't see the *Serendipity*."

Tom gave no reply but continued stare intently across the clear water off their bow, searching the shifting patterns for an indication of better air. Rick readjusted his crossed legs beneath the hiking strap, using it as an excuse to sit up momentarily and allow his burning stomach a rest from the strain lying prone over the side. He felt an arm suddenly across his chest push him backward.

Jack shook his head slightly in reproach. "Better me than him telling you to hike," he whispered.

"Tighten the cunningham," Tom stated flatly.

Rick shot his friend a withering glare as he sat up once more and leaned in to the cockpit for the sail adjustment line.

"What's happening below us?"

Rick gave a quick yank on the line and looked across the leeward water. "Three boats still on starboard, all below us." He knew enough to keep his answers short and to the point this early in the race, when the skipper's attention was fixed on weighing the best tactical decision. He moved cautiously back to the windward gunwale and maneuvered himself into the hiking straps once more.

They stayed on this heading for nearly five minutes, taking advantage of a slight shift in the wind that allowed their course to lift closer to the windward mark. Beneath, the water yellowed slightly as they left the deep basin of the middle bay and neared the western shore, with the wind easing slightly at their approach.

Tom noticed the leeward telltale on the main go slack, and he adjusted course a little to port to compensate for the new shift. He cast a quick glance over his shoulder to see the white hull in the distance on the other side of the course. "He's on our heading now and may get into this same shift. We need to go now and hope this brings us up above him. Ready about?"

They executed another tack and settled into the new heading, taking advantage of the favored course as they neared the rhumb line for their final leg to the mark. Both boys smiled at one another when they saw the *Horizon* in the distance off their starboard bow. "Looks like they're getting knocked," Rick said excitedly.

Jack noticed their own heading creep two degrees counterclockwise on the compass. "We've caught a little lift," he said evenly.

Tom looked back at the trailing salmon boat, a couple hundred yards upwind on the original tack from the line. He allowed his gaze to sweep to the right, judging the water nearer the mark. "Maury's coming into more air, and it looks like it will lift us close to where we need to go." He gave another calculating glance at the compass. "This is about to play itself out. We need to cover the *Horizon*. Ready about."

They tacked again, keeping the white hull trailing their stern a hundred yards behind. Ahead, an orange buoy bobbed a few degrees off their bow almost thirty boat lengths away. Jack's eyes darted back and forth between the telltales and the compass. The trailing thread behind the sail dipped slightly as it faltered in the changing air. "It's shifting around a little," he said calmly.

Tom moved the tiller a tiny bit to port, letting the bow edge closer to the wind. Rick saw the buoy shift slowly from right to left on the approach as they took advantage of the favorable lift. "Forty seconds to the mark," he stated. "Do you see it?"

Tom nodded stoically. "I'm going to pinch a little so we clear. Jack, keep an eye to stern. I'm sure he's seen our lift and will try to sail into this shift. Rick, get the chute ready."

Rick lowered himself slowly onto the bench and reached up into the hull space below the foredeck, taking hold of the puffy sail bag he'd stored after the end of the last race. He pulled it into the open space beside the centerboard trunk and removed the two clews and the head from the bag, letting the three corners flop outside, leaving the remaining sail stuffed within. He reached again below deck for the spinnaker pole and it held in his left hand as his right grabbed the sheet line along the starboard side and inserted it into the clawed loop in the pole's end by way of a release cable that ran the length. He quickly reached for the tension line, affixed to a small ring several feet up on the mast and connected it to the pole's midpoint then used the lower cable to open the other end, connecting the pole could be extended outward from the mast toward the forestay.

"The *Horizon* caught the lift and is now slightly above us," observed Jack, taking his attention momentarily from the main sail. He sensed the wind lift again slightly. "He's using it to bear off and gain speed!"

Tom jerked his head around as the *Deliverance* moved only a couple feet past the windward buoy on their port side. The white hull had taken full advantage of the second shift to bear off slightly toward the mark with their crew working feverishly to raise the spinnaker now that their boat had begun to pick up speed.

"Ease off Jack," barked Tom, pushing the tiller to the right and sweeping the bow around the mark toward the open water near the island's tip in the distance. "Get the chute up!"

As quickly as he could, Rick reached across to the leeward side and eased the jib sheet for the new heading then scrambled up onto the pitching deck to retrieve the spinnaker lines, held together by a common connector. He pulled them both back into the boat and separated them, making sure to connect the downwind sheet line to the correct triangle clew sticking out of the sail bag and then connected the line to one of the other triangles.

"Hurry up, Rick!" Jack pleaded. His friend had

already eased the main sail and waited nervously to take in the spinnaker lines once the big sail was quickly raised. "The *Horizon's* chute just went up!" he shouted.

Tom eyed the jibe mark a half mile distant off the island's tip, trying to decide whether to take a direct line or play a tactical move upwind slightly to keep his rival from blanketing his wind. "Keep an eye on him Jack," he commanded. "Let me know if he –"

"He's coming above us," Jack interrupted.

Rick removed the halyard from the mast and stepped back into the cockpit, working desperately to make the final connection to the sail's head before withdrawing several handfuls of sail from the bag and pushing the loose bundle toward the leeward foredeck. "Ready!"

"Go! Go!" Jack shouted.

Rick yanked downward hand over hand on the line and watched as the sail head lifted quickly up the mast. The two clew corners caught the following wind and nearly exploded outward in a billowing kaleidoscope of white, yellow and blue striping. Jack immediately pulled the guy line on the windward side and brought the clew in contact with the spinnaker pole, both arcing several feet clockwise in front of the bow. He quickly cleated the rope and used the sheet line to trim the big sail's leeward side.

Instantly the three felt the *Deliverance* gain speed.

"Raise the board one half," Tom commanded.

Jack's attention was focused solely on keeping the sail trimmed for maximum power.

Rick reached for the centerboard line in the cockpit's mid section and gave it several pulls through the cleat.

They all heard the clapping staccato of the white

—
17

boat against the waves as it bore down upon them from slightly upwind and a few boat lengths behind. Jack felt the spinnaker go slightly limp as they began to feel the effect of being blanketed.

"He's almost on top of us."

Tom glanced quickly over his shoulder to see if the *Horizon* had come into view. "Get ready to let the pole forward a little and trim the chute. When his bow gets square against our transom, I'm going to take him up a little."

Their spinnaker began to falter even more as the white hull came nearer and stole their wind. Their lead had vanished to nearly nothing as the *Horizon* had taken advantage of the blanketing tactic and now bore down upon them with notable speed. They would either use their speed and attempt to pass below them or continue on to windward, taking advantage of the blanket until they cleared the *Deliverance's* bow. When it became evident their skipper chose the latter, Tom shouted a warning to the *Horizon's* skipper. "We're coming up, Dave!"

Jack felt the bow pitch slightly as they turned several degrees to starboard. He snapped the clew line free from the cleat and played out several inches until the spinnaker pole rested nearly against the boat's forward stay while at the same time drawing in the sheet. The effect was to pivot the entire spinnaker mass counter clockwise in relation to the boat's heading, allowing Tom to steer the boat on closer reach. "Coming up!" Tom shouted again, taking advantage of the rules which favored their downwind position, requiring the upwind boat to adjust its course. He then lowered his voice and regarded both boys meaningfully. "Get ready to fall off quickly."

Jack nodded as he continued to monitor the sail

trim.

Within moments, the *Horizon* responded to windward to match course, keeping their blanket advantage as they continued to overtake the *Deliverance's* yellow hull. Rick ducked his head and looked beneath the spinnaker's foot, spotting the jibe mark now at eleven o'clock off their own bow.

The move had cost them the lead but had gained them clear air once again. Though the *Horizon* had now pulled slightly ahead, it no longer had the tactical advantage of the blanket. Jack felt their spinnaker respond and fill fully, bringing their hull on a matching speed a half boat length behind and slightly downwind. The two hulls were only a dozen feet apart, pushing quickly across the waves on a course above the rhumb line to the jibe mark.

Well to their stern, the remaining fleet followed a direct path to the mark, forming a line of white sails and colorful spinnakers racing one after the other. With each passing second, the pair's lead eroded in what had become a game of cat and mouse away from the most direct course.

"Where you taking us Tom?" shouted the opposing skipper, clearly frustrated by his inability to do anything but wait for the *Deliverance* to make its move.

Tom looked stealthily over toward the next mark, now almost perpendicular off their port side in the distance. "Ten seconds," he said quietly to the boys. "When I give the word, we fall off to run. Jack, bring the chute around quickly, and be prepared for him to cover. Rick, when he starts to make his move, you get the pole ready to jibe."

Rick's felt his heart beat in his chest. The jibe required a precision he'd never felt comfortable in doing, particularly in this situation where speed was critical.

Since he was the smaller of the two boys, he was naturally chosen as the fore crew, because he could move more easily onto the deck and because his lower weight wouldn't impact the heel as much. His eyes lifted to the skipper's face.

"We need it smooth, you understand?" Tom said encouragingly, giving a quick nod and looking once more toward the mark. "Now boys. Let's go." He quickly eased the main sheet as he pushed the tiller windward and brought the boat suddenly away from the wind on a new course that ran just to right of the jibe mark on a dead run. At once, Jack released the spinnaker lines and began to pull the sail clockwise until the chute ran full in front of their bow.

The *Horizon* reacted almost immediately and adjusted its course, but the delay caused them to sweep in a wider arc so that they ended up on a parallel run fifty feet off the *Deliverance's* starboard side. To their left, the line of four boats came ever nearer, each moving more quickly on the direct broad reach to the approaching buoy.

Rick scrambled cautiously onto the foredeck and struggled to unhook the spinnaker pole from the mast. He pivoted it across, keeping the other end attached to the guy line while he tried to reconnect the free end to the taut sheet off the port end. Their downwind heading put the bow directly into the running waves, causing the bow to pitch and roll as the hull lifted above each crest and descended into the trough.

Tom judged the mark's approach, now only a hundred yards ahead and slowly passing to their left. "Prepare to jibe." He looked quickly to the left and saw the advancing fleet, their crews also reading to jibe around the mark. "It's going to be close," he pressed. "Rick, get that pole set, now!"

Rick struggled to keep his balance and hold the release cable while trying to catch the chute's sheet line in the open connector.

"The *Horizon* has pulled wide and is trying to jibe," Jack said, watching their rival's movements as he waited.

Tom couldn't wait any longer. He reached over and grabbed the main sheet as he started to push the tiller to the right. "We have to go. Ready, jibe."

Jack instantly began to shift the spinnaker clockwise before the boat, playing out the sheet in his left hand as his right took up the slack. He ducked instinctively when he saw Tom reach up and help the boom across the cockpit as the main sail filled and shifted violently over to starboard. "C'mon, Rick," he pleaded.

"I'm trying!" the boy shouted, nearly falling over when the bow shifted onto its new heading. He yanked the near side of the release cable and removed the pole's other end from the starboard spinnaker line, making it easier without any tension to connect the far end to the new guy line. He opened the claw once more and thrust the pole into position, catching the line in one motion as he lifted the near end up and onto the mast, setting the pole in its proper place. "Got it!"

Jack adjusted the lines to bring the pole against the forestay. "It's going to be close," he said to Rick, who had scrambled back into the cockpit and looked frazzled.

With thirty yards to go, the fleet approached from their left on the opposite port tack toward the mark. "Starboard!" shouted Tom again as the lead boat approached their common goal.

"Hold your course!" came the reply.

Tom knew he was clear of the trailing three boats, but the lead boat *Serendipity* was converging quickly.

"Jibe around," they heard their skipper shout when they had cleared the *Deliverance's* bow by only a dozen feet. Instantly, the *Serendipity* came around in a tight pivot at the buoy, losing speed as their mainsail flew across the deck. Rick watched the blonde-haired girl deftly shift the pole from one side to the other in almost perfect execution, allowing their middle crew to quickly trim the spinnaker.

"Let it go," Jack teased him, seeing their sail began to take shape on the new heading.

The *Deliverance* nearly ran into the *Serendipity's* stern as she passed the mark.

"Pole forward!" Tom said deliberately, adjusting their course above their hull in a passing reach. "I want to stay above the fleet as we head for the line."

The girl had resumed her spot in the cockpit and looked over to Rick with an expression of fear. "That was close," she mouthed.

As if he read her mind, the *Serendipity's* skipper called over his shoulder in a playful tone. "How about that, Tom?"

"How's about your move now, Peter," he shouted in return, feeling the *Deliverance* angle slightly higher to windward to gain clear air. Then in a softer voice, "He's got the Horizon just below him going for the line. He'll have to decide whether to cover Dave's boat or worry about us."

Jack took his attention away from the spinnaker trim and sighted across the bow. "The pin's directly ahead. What's the plan?"

"We hope Peter tries to cover the *Horizon* to slow her down as we near it. Let's ease off a little and do the same to them." He reached down and let out a few feet of line from the mainsheet block. The *Deliverance* adjusted course and began to approach the *Serendipity* from upwind, taking advantage of the same tactic their rival was using against the *Horizon*. The three boats continued closely on parallel courses, with the *Deliverance* pulling slightly ahead to windward in the clearer air. "This won't be good enough," Tom muttered, then amended when he saw a look of bewilderment on the boy's faces. "We may be a little ahead, but with the angle of the finish line, the *Horizon's* got the clear shot across the pin. The only hope we've got is a –"

"There's air off Ingleside," Jack interrupted, causing all three to turn their heads and look upwind. A large patch of turbulent water showed itself as it came down the lake. Tom glanced over to the moored boats near the shore from where the air originated. "It's a shift. Those boats have come around clockwise." He looked back again to the approaching finish line and then swept his gaze to the rivals off his starboard side. "Better hope it's a big one."

"Two hundred yards to the line," Jack said excitedly.

Rick watched excitedly as the committee pontoon also began to swing around in the new air. Its stern formed a slight angle with the imaginary finish line. "Here it comes!"

The puff came violently across their port bow, immediately causing the spinnaker and main to falter in the large change of direction. "It's a big knock!" Tom shouted as he thrust the tiller to windward to bring their heading back onto a reach toward the line. He swung his head around. "Jack and Dave got it too." The *Deliverance* began to heel significantly in the stronger air. "Get her flat boys!"

The shift caused all three boats to adjust course to maintain speed, rotating in sync so that the

Serendipity now moved in parallel beside *Deliverance's* starboard beam, a half boat length behind. The Horizon lay on a similar course off the *Serendipity's* hull with all three racing for the approaching finish.

A plume of spray shot up from the bow and hit Rick full on in the face, blinding him momentarily. He turned his head toward Jack who lay straining beside him, both grinning wildly as the *Deliverance's* hull started to hum across the choppy water.

"Hike for those turkey dinners, boys!" Tom shouted wildly, pointing with his free hand toward the Horizon two boats over, seeing their sails falter in the dirty air.

The remaining hundred yards were a blur of wind and water and breathless noise as the *Serendipity* and *Deliverance* thrust ahead neck and neck, crossing the line nearly together as they surged past the orange pin. The boys shouted enthusiastically, and Tom gave a thumbs-up to his rivals. Two staccato blasts emerged from the bullhorn, signaling both boats had successfully crossed the line together.

The three waited nervously as the woman on the committee boat brought the horn to her lips. "One-three-one-seven-four. Over." Jack and Rick hollered in celebration at hearing their sail number called first. "One-two-two-six-three. Over," she broadcast immediately thereafter.

"Nicely done, boys," Tom said, lifting a hand once again and waving toward the *Serendipity*. He let their boat arc gently to port to slow down as the sails began to flap wildly. "Let's get the chute down and reset the jib."

The *Horizon* had crossed the line several seconds behind and came alongside below the Deliverance. "Took us on a little tour there, eh Tom?"

Dave said jokingly.

Tom laughed and stuck a thumb windward, gesturing toward the open waves out near Ingleside. The moored boats had swung back to their original position, and a new pattern of crisscrossed water came steadily toward them. "Just lucky, I guess!" he shouted as two more horns signaled the arrival of the rest of the fleet.

Rick dismantled the pole and let down the chute, cautiously stuffing it into the waiting sail bag at the edge of the cockpit. He watched as his friend reset the lines and lowered the centerboard in its trunk. "Want to trade places?" he said teasingly, though Jack sensed there was something more.

"You did just fine," he replied, nodding to the jib halyard. "Besides, you get all the fun stuff. Setting the sails, scrambling on the deck, working the pole –"

"Struggling to jibe the pole, more like it." Rick yanked down on the jib halyard and watched as the white sail lifted upward from foredeck. He affixed the retaining wire into the mast and stepped backward carefully in to the cockpit.

His friend gave him an empathetic smile. "There's no way I could balance up there and juggle everything. Like I said, you did just fine."

"The wind's coming up a little," Tom said as they neared the shallower water off Ingleside. "You boys ready about? Start looking for the signal any moment."

They tacked over and began sailing close hauled toward the line, feeling the boat heel noticeably in the building air. Tom chuckled suddenly and gave the boys a knowing grin. "Get ready to go around again. And Rick, it's going to be faster at the jibe mark if this wind holds." He laughed warmly and nodded for them to get upward on the gunwale to hike out. "Anyway," he added, lifting himself up and hooking his feet underneath straps to lean out. "It doesn't get much better than this."

Chapter 2

Present Day

The two-lane road meandered through thick woods and in and out of open fields, following south along the curving bluffs high above lake Michigan to the west. Heather leaned her head out the passenger window and glanced upward at the tunnel of trees overhead, admiring the shifting mosaic of green among patches here and there where the blue sky poked through the dense canopy. Turning her face toward him, she said softly, "This is wonderful."

Rick's brow furrowed slightly. "I thought you said you'd been here before?"

She nodded and returned her attention to the woods. "I have. It was a couple of years ago when I first came to the Bug Camp. Charles was kind enough to take me on an afternoon tour."

Rick wondered for a moment if giving tours was something the Director was supposed to do for new faculty hires, a responsibility the departing Charles never mentioned to him during his retirement transition from the Biological Station last year.

Heather easily read his thoughts. "I bet you're wondering if *you* were supposed to –"

"That's enough."

She turned her head once again to him. "You mean you didn't even have the decency to give Lydia the grand tour when she arrived? What kind of Director are you, Professor Parsons?"

Rick admired the play of light and shadows on her face as she regarded him teasingly. His attention diverted momentarily when they came to a spot where the road curved sharply and descended a small hill. A cyclist going in the opposite direction rounded the corner too quickly, veered dangerously into their oncoming path, and recovered in time to avoid a collision.

"That's the fourth one since Cross Village," Heather said.

Rick watched the cyclist retreat in his rear view mirror. "Sunday's worse. There's a big pack of them, maybe thirty or so, that go out of Harbor Springs every Sunday morning and ride M119 up to Cross Village and then turn around and head back. It'd be one thing if they stayed together the whole way, but they get strung out after several miles, and it's tough for drivers to share the narrow road."

"Is that what you meant before by there being bikers on the road?"

He chuckled softly. "Not exactly. M119 is also popular with the motorcycle crowd."

"As in biker gangs?" Her expression looked mildly concerned.

The chuckle turned into a full laugh, mostly because of the way her Irish accent made it sound musically like 'biker ging.' "It's not like a pack of Hell's Angels descending on Northern Michigan," he replied, steering the car up the ascending hill and turning once again onto an undulating stretch through the woods. "A good many of them are well-to-do types from downstate or around Chicago, come north to get away from their high-end jobs. They don the entire biker get up of leather jackets and jeans and ride along these scenic roads."

"I can tell from your tone you don't approve."

"I just think it's a bit ridiculous, that's all." Rick jerked a thumb toward the road behind them. "Remind me to take you to dinner on a Friday or Saturday back in Cross Village at Legs Inn." He shook his head derisively. "Those weekday stockbrokers roll into Cross Village on a Friday afternoon like packs of would-be Hellions. It sort of takes away from the atmosphere, if you ask me."

It was Heather's turn to chuckle.

"What?"

"You don't seem to criticize the cycling crowd?" she said with a bemused expression.

"Didn't I just say they make driving along here complicated?"

"I didn't mean that. I was referring to their outfits." She gestured meaningfully out the windshield.

At that moment, another lone cyclist came whizzing from the opposite direction. Rick barely had time to catch sight of his colorful Lycra skin suit and shaved legs as he passed by. His lips pursed momentarily as he considered a counter argument.

She raised her voice accusingly. "You not seriously going to tell me there's any difference?"

The pucker turned into a sheepish grin, and he turned to face her. "I guess you might say they look a little ridiculous too."

"It's all a matter of perspective. As I recall you told me once you used to think the Bug Camp researchers were a little nerdy."

"Point taken."

The road emerged into more open land as they entered the outskirts of the small village of Good Hart, the site of what was formerly a Native American gathering place along the bluffs and down beside the lakeshore a couple hundred yards to the west. To their right, the trees thinned enough to allow them glimpses of the blue expanse of Lake Michigan far below, and Rick slowed the car as they approached a group of several buildings in the village center.

Rick pointed at a squarish red building with white trim next to the road. From its front roof edge hung a string of patriotic bunting over a plain white sign that read 'General Store'. "You ever been in –"

"Yes, a couple years ago," Heather replied meaningfully.

Rick sighed. "Let me guess. Part of Charles' tour?" He turned the car into the small parking lot next to the building.

"As I recall," she added, "they had some yummy baked goods inside," Her eyes searched through the windshield and found the small log cabin tucked beside the General Store set back into the woods. "just in case this doesn't work out."

Rick unbuckled and began to open his door. "You know, for a plant biologist, you are remarkably queasy about being adventurous with eating."

"All I'm saying is that I'm glad the General Store is here in case our idea of local cuisine is a little different than Jan's."

Rick stood and peered down into the car, taking note that she had yet to even unfasten her belt. "If it makes you feel better, I did a quick search on the internet to see the reviews of this place, in case Jan was trying to play a practical joke."

"And?" She remained steadfastly glued to the passenger seat.

"And, the owner has received some exceptional reviews. It's even passed muster with the Harbor Springs crowd."

Heather raised her hands theatrically. "Oh, well then! If it's good enough for Harbor Springs, it must surely be good enough for us Bug Camp peasants." She began to unfasten then hesitated, turning her gaze once more to the log cabin. "Looks a little primitive."

Rick shook his head. "You are a very mysterious woman, Heather Wilkins! You don't seem to mind the rusticity of the biological station at all. I get you off the reservation, however, and you turn a little –"

"Don't." She gave him a stern warning. "You can't blame a girl for wanting a fancy eatery now and then. The Bug Camp is one thing, but this is an official date." She opened her door and got out. "Besides, I like it that you find your fiancé a little mysterious." Her mouth formed a sly grin, and she turned and walked directly toward the cabin, not waiting for him to follow.

#

The dining area was a single room, roughly twenty feet square with wide pine floors and a post and beam design overhead. A large wood-burning stove occupied the center with a chimney pipe that extended upward into the white ceiling. The walls were tastefully adorned with various pieces of Odawa artwork, interspersed with prints of native wildflowers and scenes of northern Michigan. Two tables sat beneath a large picture window providing a view toward the bluff escarpment that descended from the forest toward lake Michigan below. Where the exterior of the cabin was rustic to the point of neglect, the inside of the Good Earth Restaurant was altogether charming.

"You both look a little surprised." A dark-haired woman who wore a peasant skirt and simple blue blouse stood next to their table, appraising them with dark eyes and an almost cherubic face.

Heather's attention was fixed on a small shelf next to where the owner had seated them. It contained three large quill boxes, each made from the bark of white birch trees and covered in decorative patterns with porcupine quills, finished with a band of twilled sweet grass around the edges.

Rick smiled. "You've decorated this space beautifully."

"Thank you," she replied. "Most of the pieces here come from local artisans."

Heather glanced up. "These are wonderful."

The woman nodded. "Those are quill boxes. There are only a handful of Odawa people left who still do them. These three were made by my Aunt, who lives a few miles south of here."

Heather suddenly registered what the woman said earlier. "Did you say we looked a little surprised?"

The woman smiled again. "I did. Let me guess. A combination of the rough exterior and the thought of eating foraged cuisine?" Their sheepish expressions confirmed her suspicion. "As for the exterior, this old cabin is nearly a hundred years old, and I wanted to keep it as close to the original condition as possible. It actually is on the registry for historic buildings in the village, and so while the outside must partially adhere to the town sentiments, the inside belongs solely to my own tastes." She glanced about the room as if seeing it for the first time. "Which, I suppose is arguably a reflection of the original peoples along this shore anyway." Her eyes settled on them. "My family dates back to the time of the Middle Village."

"Poneshing?" Rick asked.

"The very same. My great grandfather, thrice removed was Joseph Poneshing, and he also lived in the

Middle Village, not far from where the St. Ignatius church is located near the shore."

"And Bethany?"

"Not exactly Odawa, I grant you, but neither was Joseph. So that's me, Bethany Poneshing, and allow me to welcome you formerly to my restaurant the Good Earth. Since you are both new, shall I give you the brief bio? I assume you have an interest in either local food or the idea of foraging?"

"We're from the Biological Station on Douglas Lake," Rick offered.

"The Bug Camp!" Beth replied enthusiastically.

Heather looked impressed. "You know of us?"

"Of course I am familiar with the Bug Camp. Wonderful place. Are you both faculty?"

Rick nodded and gestured to Heather. "This is Heather Wilkins, who teaches courses in Ecology and Evolutionary Palynology." Heather smiled. "And I'm Rick Parsons. I'm the new Director at the Station, and I teach a course in Freshwater Algae and another having to do with the study of Bryophytes."

Beth's eyes widened slightly. "I assume you are the same Erasmus Parsons who was involved with the case on the Maple River a couple years ago?"

Rick's face became guarded. "Yes. That's correct. I helped assist the Cheboygan Police with some of the forensic work on the murder."

"That was a nasty affair. That poor woman," she said simply. "And yet, it seems they went ahead with the dam removal on the river anyway. The Little Traverse Odawa were certainly pleased."

"Ah," Rick said, recalling how the local Band of Odawa was consulted during the feasibility phase of the removal of the dam across the Maple River. "I assume you're a part of their membership?"

33

She laughed. "Of course, but my interest in the restoration was mostly professional." She gestured around the room to emphasize her point. "I do some seasonal foraging in the woods bordering both branches of the Maple River. Mushrooms mostly, when the conditions are favorable. I learned about the dam removal from a friend of mine a couple years ago. She was the one who told me about your work."

Rick shook his head as Heather gave a soft chuckle. "Let me guess, Jan Fowler at the Brutus Camp Deli?"

Beth beamed. "One and the same! She told me she's known you since you were kids."

"Jan was the person who suggested that we come here for lunch," Heather said. "She said ... how did she put it Rick?"

"That we were only pretend plant biologists if we weren't adventurous enough to try your specialty." He looked to Heather for confirmation.

"It was something like that, only more colorful if I remember correctly."

Rick laughed. "More colorful alright. She did say you have an amazing way of cooking with local plants. I've read a few articles about your work. You've received some high praise and evidently have a following from the Harbor and Petoskey crowds."

"That's very kind of you to say," Beth replied. At that moment, two women entered the door and stood waiting for attention. "Would you mind excusing me for a moment while I get them seated? They've both been here for lunch several times before, and I suspect they'll order what I tend to recommend this time of the summer. I'll be back in just a moment."

Heather watched her cross the room and engage the seated pair. "Just another person who knows you as the one and only Erasmus Parsons."

He winced slightly then sighed. "You know, one of these days I'm going to give up and just start insisting that everyone call me by my Christian name."

"I think it gives you distinction," she quipped.

"You just like getting under my skin."

Her expression turned mischievous. "That, and other things I like doing with you." Her eyes then widened. "What about asking her?"

Rick was completely baffled. "What? You want me to ask her about using my full name or about our love life?"

"No, silly! About giving a talk at the Camp. You told me earlier today Peg was having a difficult time finding a replacement for the speaker who had to pull out."

His face relaxed, and he shook his head. "Go figure. You can switch between playful teasing to Camp business in the blink of an eye."

She shrugged. "Well?"

"It's not a bad idea. What are you thinking? Edible and medicinal wild plants around Douglas Lake?"

"It may encourage other lake residents to attend. I bet it would be a good turn out."

They both looked up at Beth's return. "Would you like to see the menu of what I have available today, or can I convince you to try one of my specialty preparations?"

Rick saw Heather nod to him encouragingly. "Beth." He hesitated. "May I call you Beth?"

"Of course, if you don't mind Erasmus."

Heather giggled.

Rick silenced her with an icy glare. "Rick will do just fine. Preferable, actually. The formal name has been an unfortunate albatross from my parents."

35

Beth looked to Heather for explanation, but she just shrugged.

"First, we're here, partly because our mutual friend Jan told us to be a little adventurous. So, feel free to indulge yourself on our account, so long as it's nothing too exotic or borderline – ". He stopped short, not sure how best to put it.

"Borderline as in dangerous, you mean," Beth added.

Rick let out a muffled laugh. "Well, yes, I guess."

She looked back and forth between them. "I assure you nothing overly exotic. In fact, you may be surprised, perhaps even disillusioned that I use some rather common foraged items." She winked then. "However, I think you will be impressed."

"That was the consensus of the reviews I've read," Rick said. "And second, we were wondering if you had any interest in giving a talk at the Biological Station as a part of our summer colloquium series."

Heather leaned in. "The Bug Camp prides itself on its wide range of weekly seminar talks in which various experts and scholars speak to students, faculty and surrounding residents about their interests. Rick and I were just discussing how a talk about locally foraged plants would go over very well with the students. We know it's short notice, but we have an opening in a couple weeks on a Friday evening."

"I'd be happy to share my experience with your group," Beth beamed. "In fact, I'm giving a similar thing to local group hosted by the Outfitter down in Harbor Springs this Saturday. Mostly, I'll talk about some of the ways various Little Traverse wildflowers and perennials could be used in both culinary and medicinal contexts. Sort of a dos and don'ts of foraging, if you will."

Rick remembered her earlier comment about

picking mushrooms along the Maple River. "I imagine you have to be careful to emphasize what not to pick and eat as much as anything."

Beth nodded soberly. "Quite true. Although I love sharing my experience with the public, I'm almost paranoid about pointing out the potential dangers in foraging. I assure you I'd highlight that with your audience at the Camp. Did you say Friday in two weeks?"

Rick nodded. "The Friday after next. This would give us time to properly advertise. The Biological Station has a close relationship with a group of conservation-minded citizens along the shores of Douglas Lake called the D.L.I.A."

"Douglas Lake Improvement Association," Heather added for clarification.

"We'll make sure to tell their members about your talk, and that will drum up a large group of the general public. And," he added, raising his eyebrows meaningfully, "it could be good for your business here to tap into more customers."

Beth's expression became slightly troubled. "I'm sorry. I have a conflict with that particular Friday. It's the weekend of the Little Traverse Regatta and the Annual Taste of Harbor Festival. I'll be running a booth for the Festival out on the common from Friday afternoon through the following day and then helping with the banquet preparations Saturday evening. Is there any chance I could do the talk a week later?"

"Hmm," Rick said. "We have another speaker coming the following week to talk about climate change." He looked at Heather to see if she had any objections. "I can't think of any reason why we couldn't move the seminar talk to the day before."

"Just check with Peg to see if the Gates Hall is free," Heather said.

"How about Thursday?" Rick said to her hopefully.

Beth's expression brightened. "Thursday it is. A big lecture hall you say?" Both guests nodded. "So if I brought an electronic file with images to show, you'd have a projector on site?"

"If that would be easier for you."

"I'll also gather some local samples to show. Most of what I'll discuss will be common enough, but it's always nice to have some fresh material on hand. Plus, if I have a chance, I'll try to do a little exploration around Douglas sometime next week and see if I can locate some of the likely places for the less common species."

"Then it's settled," Heather said. "Thank you for agreeing to come."

Beth smiled and began to turn toward the far wall, where a door led into what they assumed was the back kitchen area. "And now, I need some time to prepare your not-too-adventurous meal." She winked and called over her shoulder as she left them. "Though you can tell Jan it was as adventurous as you like."

#

Rick's mouth began to water when Beth placed two identical plates in front of them. "The main dish is my pan-seared whitefish with a light coating of butter and seasoned with a dusting of wild fennel pollen." She turned and gathered two smaller plates from the waiting tray behind her. "This is a Purslane salad with olive oil and garlic croutons."

"Oooh," Heather said as the salad plate was placed next to the main dish. "It smells wonderful."

Rick's eyebrows went up. "This grows next to the administration building where the runoff from the roof collects near the gravel lot."

Beth laughed. "Purslane is a fairly common weed, and it loves neglected places with good sun exposure like vacant lots or farmland. I begin harvesting the tender clusters in mid June when it starts to get large enough, and I can keep going back for more tips throughout the remainder of the summer. It has a nice crunchy texture and is high in omega 3."

"I'm about to eat parking lot weeds," Rick said drily.

"Some people who know Purslane worry about oxalic acid in them, but really there's no real cause for concern."

"Calcium depletion?" Heather asked casually. Rick's mouth opened slightly in surprise.

"Correct, but you'd have to eat pounds of the stuff to cause any real problems."

Rick tried to visualize eating pounds of parking lot weeds.

"And finally," she continued, reaching for the remaining plate which contained several slices of bread. "My bread recipe using acorn flower." She noticed Heather about to comment. "I know," she added, raising her hand palm outward in defense. "No acorns. Not yet, anyway. The flour for this batch came from nuts I gathered and dried last autumn."

Rick immediately reached for a slice of bread and took a tentative bite, expecting it to be slightly bitter. "This is wonderful. It's kind of – " he paused, unable to think of anything else but "nutty tasting."

Heather gave him a look that conveyed something along the lines of *you've got to be kidding*.

Beth smiled. "The secret is to thoroughly soak the nuts in clean water after you roast them. It usually requires a couple weeks, and I try to change the water at least once a day to remove the tannins. I have a several large red oak trees in my front yard, and in a good mast year I can gather enough to make almost twenty pounds of flour."

Rick pointed to the fish. "And the fennel?"

"Is quite versatile. Almost all of it is edible, from the seeds and roots to the yellow flowers, which can be sprinkled into greens or turned into desserts. Of course, the pollen has a more limited time for gathering, but you'll find it, like the rest of the plant, contains the distinctive anise odor and flavor."

Heather had already taken a bite of fish and now looked admirably at their host. "This is simply delicious," she mumbled as she savored the warm flavors.

"I'm pleased you think so." Beth turned once more to leave them to enjoy their meal. "I hope you find the parking lot weeds equally so."

#

Heather watched him use the last slice of bread to mop up the remaining fennel butter. "I have to admit, that was great," Rick said.

"What do you know about the Taste of Harbor Festival?"

"It used to be a large farmer's market years ago in Zoll Park." Heather's forehead bunched together. "You remember where we parked that time we took the kayaks out into Little Traverse Bay?"

"I remember the water was freezing for mid July. Do you mean that place near where the road goes along the shore?"

"That's it. The big grassy park used to host a farmer's market in early August. It's probably been twenty years since the last one."

"And the Festival?"

"I think the market morphed into a more upscale event which became the Taste of Harbor. The town's been running it for at least the past dozen years on the common by the Pier Restaurant. It takes place on the weekend of the Little Traverse Regatta, when the place is packed to the gills with the Nouveau riche and the yachting crowd." He stopped when he saw the smirk on her face. "What?"

"Sounds like you have something against Harbor Springs?"

"It has its good points," he said neutrally. "The town itself is beautiful, and I have good memories of going there to watch the Fourth of July fireworks when I was in my late teens. It's just the summer people I can't stomach."

"Meaning?"

His eyes narrowed. "I think you're baiting me. I know full well you've gotten the scoop from Jan what it was like for her to grow up as a local in Harbor. Plus, I saw the expression on your face when we drove through the town last time."

Heather remembered feeling conspicuously out of place as they drove her old dusty Subaru up the main street, past the spotless BMWs, Mercedes and Land Rovers parked one after another, where the well-to-do men and women strolled the sidewalks like living incarnations of Barbie and Ken. "I remember feeling a little out of place," she replied.

"They're nice enough," he allowed, "but the whole place is a caricature of snobbery."

It suddenly occurred to her that there was something deeper with his feelings, but she decided not to press. "What about the regatta?"

He was thankful for the slight change in topic.

"It's become a fairly prestigious race. I think they draw somewhere between twenty and thirty boats for the two day event. If it's like the old days, they run two races on Saturday and two on Sunday, with the combined finish places determining the overall boat placements. It used to be just a single class race, but they opened it up as a mixed series a long time ago."

Heather recognized something in his voice about the 'old days'. "You've done it?"

Rick leaned back and nodded. "Long time ago. At least twenty five years. Remember how I said a bunch of us grew up sailing on Douglas?"

"Yes."

"Well, every once in a while we'd get the opportunity to crew for some of the bigger boats out of Harbor or Charlevoix. I got to serve as a boat weight one time for the Little Traverse."

Heather cocked her head. "Boat weight?"

Rick chuckled. "Yeah. Means I didn't do much more than just move around the boat when they needed a little weight to keep the hull from heeling."

"Sounds a little boring."

He shrugged. "It was still fun to be in the big league for a change. A good friend who started crewing with me on Douglas ended up switching over to the Harbor races full time." Rick laughed. "He was no boat weight like me. He was an excellent sailor and at one time a very good friend."

Again, she detected something interconnected but decided not to press. "How come you've never taken me?"

"Taken you where?"

"Sailing, silly. What did you think I meant?"

He shrugged and then looked at her inquisitively. "Do you want to try sailing? The Camp's got a couple of old Sunfishes down by the Lakeside Lab. We could rig one of them and go out when the wind's not too strong."

Heather pictured the diminutive size of the Sunfish cockpit and tried to imagine how cramped it would be whizzing along with him across the bay. "Would we get wet?"

He grinned slyly. "Probably."

"What about tipping over?"

The grin turned into a devilish smile. "Could be. Depends on the wind and other things."

"What other things?" she asked dubiously.

He laughed then. "Like whether or not you make a good boat weight."

Her mouth formed a rueful expression. "Well then, there's nothing like being called a boat weight to get a girl to try sailing. When do we go?"

Chapter 3

Jack pushed the clutch as they emerged from the woods into a sharp right curve, narrowly avoiding a group of joggers who hastily jumped out of the way onto the shoulder. They glared at them with a mixture of anger and admiration, the latter toward the beautiful Austin Healey that nearly bowled them over. He downshifted and reengaged, feeling the roadster pitch with the turn, much in the way his boat heeled over with a change in heading. The road ahead followed a gentle arc along the shoreline of Little Traverse Bay, visible in places through narrow gaps in the border trees.

"Are you satisfied how that went?" he spoke evenly, thankful for the distraction the view provided. When she didn't respond for several seconds, he looked over. "Did you hear me?"

Veronica stared stoically ahead through the windshield, her porcelain complexion revealing nothing of her feelings. She detested how the wind came in a constant eddy from behind the convertible, pulling repeatedly at loose strands of her ebony hair, which somehow escaped from beneath the scarf she'd tied around her head when they'd left the therapist's office. She reached up and methodically adjusted the oversized sunglasses back onto the bridge of her nose, not bothering to turn in his direction. "I don't think satisfied is the correct word," she replied coolly.

A hint of irritation crept into his voice. "Look,

Ronnie." He saw the corner of her mouth twitch slightly, and he smiled inwardly, knowing how she disliked the nickname. "I agreed to go, didn't I?" He shifted into a higher gear and accelerated around a gentle curve. "I mean, what do you expect?"

"You agreed," she said, "only because my father insisted we go through with it. Don't insult me by insinuating anything else."

The road reentered the woods into a sweeping curve around one of many natural springs in the area. A small creek bubbled up through sandy soil and descended gently through a winding course downhill toward the bay below, and Jack felt the air temperature drop several degrees with the sudden shade, wondering if his wife's temperament somehow made it more pronounced. Her sudden laughter caught him off guard. "And what is more pathetic," she continued icily, "is I've become just like her, bending to his will just like she did."

Jack thought it was ironic how Veronica could be so submissive to her father while at the same time perfectly comfortable being a bitch to him. For a moment, it occurred to him how he'd become something of a William Cabbott himself. "I guess we've both become something we didn't expect," he replied as they left the woods into bright sunlight where the road entered the outskirts of the village.

His father in-law was the epitome of what many characterized as Harbor Spring's nouveau riche, having acquired his fortune through the marriage of Veronica's mother in a hasty courtship that resulted in an only daughter. Louisa Cabbott passed away several years before Veronica and Jack were married, and though he had never had the opportunity to know her personally, Jack had learned enough throughout the years to draw his own conclusions. Louisa Cabbott was by all accounts an introverted woman and not particularly attractive, save for the large inheritance she was to receive from her family's real estate of the former farm land a mile north of the village. It was all the more ironic that William Cabbott had been raised in a rundown home on a small piece of property off State Road outside of town, next to the tracks of land which would one day become the basis of his fortune. It didn't take much imagination to know why he pursued the former Louisa Bainbridge nor why, once they had become established through the following years as new arrivals to Harbor wealth, William Cabbott's attention began to stray afield from his submissive wife.

Unlike her mother, Veronica Cabbott was an attractive and popular girl with no shortage of would-be suitors during her formative years growing up among the society of Harbor Springs. Within the coterie who conformed to blonde hair and the latest fashion and who valued ostentation because they knew no other way, Veronica stood apart from her peers. With her straight black hair and light skin, and wardrobe that suggested nothing of the wealth most within society knew her family to possess, she was something of an anomaly. And Jack was drawn to her at first sight.

During the summers between college terms, he had worked as a "gopher" for the local boat shop in Harbor, one that catered to high-end customers who spared little expense in purchasing and servicing their recreational and competitive vessels. His duties were largely menial - getting boats ready for launch at the beginning of the season, ferrying equipment to and from the yard, and assisting with clean up and inventory during those times when need required. This experience also allowed him to be around the one passion he'd had since childhood – a love of sailing and racing and the atmosphere that enveloped it.

Through his connections, he managed to serve as crew for several of the one-design races that took place throughout the season in the bay, quickly gaining a reputation as a capable sailor who had talent for racing tactics and for reading the wind. In time, he was given the chance to skipper one of Irwin's older hulls in the J series, putting together a ragtag crew of fellow employees, much in the manner of a team of talented caddies given the chance to display their own skill on a larger stage. When he successfully skippered the disadvantaged boat and rather soundly defeated several well known local crews, Jack suddenly found himself elevated within the circle of the acceptable sailing elite. He had arrived, without pedigree, but with enough talent and ambition that people began to notice. Veronica Cabbott was among them.

She had waited for him on the pier, hesitantly standing beneath the yellow beam of a can light, watching as he stowed the sails and reset the rigging on the beautiful J boat four slips out from shore and several dozen yards from where she stood. In the harbor beyond were the dark forms of dozens of crafts, their masts barely visible against the deepening indigo of the midsummer night sky. Across the bay, the narrow peninsula of Harbor Point jut outward into the open water, its tree lined shore sheltering the summer cottages of the elite.

He approached her then, carrying a large duffle bag slung over his shoulder, startled when she shifted in the light.

"You're Jack Stinson," she said confidently.

He tried to see her face clearly, but the beam above cast a shadow over her features. "That's right. I'm

Jack," he replied, lifting a hand to block the beam. "Who's there?"

She took a step closer. "Veronica Cabbott."

He had seen her before at a gathering hosted by the yacht club on the grassy common behind them where the pier thrust outward from the shore. She was pretty enough and different from the other girls in her social circle. His eyes narrowed. "Are you waiting for me?"

She barely nodded. "I saw you come across the line out there today. Did you win?"

He studied her for a moment, curious. "Second place." He saw confusion on her face. "We won the final race but took second in the series. Were you on the committee boat?"

She laughed softly and shook her head. "On my father's yacht just off the finish line. The deep cruiser."

"Ah. I should have guessed. It's a beautiful boat."

She looked down at her shoes, thinking, and then met his eyes again. "Where are you headed now?"

He deposited the heavy duffle on the wooden planks and regarded her. "Back to Irwin to return the race gear."

"And then?"

Jack lifted a hand and pointed down the pier behind her. "Supposed to wind down with the guys at Bar Harbor."

Veronica glanced toward the waterside restaurant next to where they stood. A row of cocktail tables was placed underneath a large decorative canopy along the wall facing the dock. Several well-dressed couples stood mingling with one another, each oblivious to the pair standing yards away. "I thought most crews went next door to –"

He snorted and reached down for the duffle. "To the Pier. Most do. We," he nodded again across the street, "feel more welcome over there."

She hesitated.

A slight smile played on his lips. "Care to join me?"

"Across the street?"

He nodded. "Unless you'd rather go next door. I imagine your father is there right now holding court. How many boats does he sponsor?"

She looked away. "Two, but I think you already know that." She turned to him again, her face searching. "I believe you beat them both today, which counts for something, doesn't it? I could introduce you to him, if you like."

He chuckled softly. "We've met before. I helped get his yacht ready out of storage. He was there when we launched a few months ago. I imagine he's forgotten my name as dismissively as when he shook my hand."

It was her turn to smile. "That may be, but I bet he knows who are you after this racing season. He doesn't exactly like to lose to –"

"To what? Let me guess." His face registered disgust.

Her expression remained fixed. "I was going to say that he doesn't like to lose to an outsider."

"Meaning?"

"Which means you can take it whatever way you like. Tell me again what you said before. Do you go across the street because you want to, or is it because you don't feel like you belong next door?"

He regarded her evenly. "Maybe a little of both. And why did you wait for me again?"

"Because, I've been next door my whole life, and I just want to see what's on the outside."

They both remained silent for several seconds. "You could start by joining me over there," he said finally, pointing once again across the road. He lifted the duffle to show her. "Meet back here in ten minutes, and we'll go over together?"

#

Harbor Springs is a picturesque town on the north shore of Little Traverse Bay. Its central village sits within a gentle sloping hill overlooking the turquoise water of Lake Michigan below, where several piers jut outward from the shore, and dozens of boats lay moored within the protection of the harbor. Along its eastern shore lay the historical homes of the summer resort Wequetonsing, a community formed in the late eighteen hundreds by wealthy Illinois industrialists who wanted to escape the heat and humidity of their southern residences. To the west where the bay curves sharply as it reaches toward the lighthouse on the point, private homes sit within gated communities.

In the midst of summer, the sidewalks along its main street are filled with the well to do, who mill about as much to be seen as they do to shop within one of the several boutiques and eateries that line the small village. Beyond, where the main road departs and leads along the Michigan coast, the manicured estates dwindle to pastureland and open woods as the land undulates toward the straits a dozen miles to the north.

Jack maneuvered the roadster slowly down main street, searching for an empty parking space.

"What the hell is that supposed to mean?" Veronica said.

He slowed to allow a young couple and their two children to cross the street ahead. The mother was an attractive blonde wearing a tennis outfit and holding the hand of the younger of her offspring. Neither parent

—

acknowledged them as they opened the doors to their Mercedes SUV and helped lift the two children up into the back seat before themselves getting into the car. Jack's gaze followed the mother's legs as she skirted behind her vehicle to walk around to the passenger side.

"You're a son of a bitch, you know," Veronica said bitterly, looking at him with a stony gaze. "It's been less than twenty minutes since we left the session. The least you could do is not make things worse."

He said nothing as the Mercedes pulled away from the curb and fixed his concentration on the parallel park. "What's what supposed to mean?" he said.

She blinked momentarily, still focused on his blatant distraction. "Earlier you said you'd become something you didn't expect."

He knew he'd regret the earlier comment. "Given the circumstances," he said as looked over at her, "I think we both know exactly what I meant."

She watched as a rather effeminate man dressed in multi-colored shorts and a white button down oxford shirt approached their direction from the sidewalk ahead. He held two leashes in an outstretched hand, each bearing a black toy poodle that walked obediently several steps before him. "That you're a creature of this lifestyle, like my father," she said as the man passed by. "It's easier for me to think that's what you meant."

Jack turned the key and began reaching for the door handle, wincing at her use of the word creature. "Then, that's it."

"Don't!" she said.

He sat back, defeated. "Look, Ronnie," amending when he saw her face. "Veronica, we are who we are." He thought about getting out of the car again and paused, deciding whether or not to add anything more.

"I didn't think you'd become like him," she said

with a note of sadness.

He sighed. He understood her meaning. "I wanted in, and you wanted out. Isn't that how you've always put it?"

She looked directly at him then, her expression neutral. "Well, you got what you wanted, the money, the lifestyle, the indiscretions. I guess you got in. For now."

He held her gaze for several seconds then nodded across the car toward the open doorway of the hardware store beyond. "I'll be back in a few minutes."

She said nothing and turned her head as he exited the car door.

Chapter 4

The morning sun had begun to highlight the tops of the taller pines across the water to the west. It would be another hour or so before its rays finally warmed the A-frame's expansive porch, where Rick sat idly holding a cup of coffee. A steady breeze from the northwest didn't help, coming as it did across Fishtail Bay and through the deep woods surrounding the Bug Camp, carrying the unique bouquet of summer on Douglas Lake. He rose from the worn deck chair and pulled it several feet closer near the shelter of a towering pine adjacent to the porch, content once more for the few moments of peace and quiet the Director rarely seemed to enjoy.

On the whole, he was beginning to feel that running the University Biological Station wasn't as onerous as he'd anticipated prior to the start of this summer season. When Charles had announced his retirement last autumn and recommended to the Board that Rick be appointed as his successor, he'd felt nothing but dread since, worrying whether or not he'd be up to the task. It didn't help when Peg, the Administrative Coordinator, said to him rather sarcastically, "Good gawd Rick, a trained monkey could run this place. Stop your worrying!"

The first session was nearly complete, and thankfully there had been little drama. Both the undergraduate and graduate enrollment numbers were good, and the resident faculty seemed content. Even

Professor Cummings, who typically found something to complain about, didn't present any difficulties. At least, nothing more than the usual comments from students about his somewhat prickly demeanor. He was, after all an excellent instructor, which made it easier to accept his shortcomings.

The Biological Station had been an institution on Douglas Lake for over a hundred years, having been formed initially as Camp Davis in the early nineteen hundreds, composed of a collection of rustic tents and a few ramshackle buildings along the curving bay. At the time, the lake's fifteen miles of shoreline was relatively uninhabited, apart from a couple summer cottages which had been built on a point along the north side and a scattering of abandoned Native American settlements along the south tucked within the bordering woods.

The Station had grown significantly during the intervening years, with rustic tents having been replaced by small tin cabins and with the construction of academic and lab buildings tucked aesthetically within the surrounding forest. It had gained a strong reputation for teaching and research in the natural sciences, particularly in ecology and atmospheric study, and had been hosting faculty and students consistently for decades, living in what most around the area knew affectionately as the Bug Camp.

Rick inhaled deeply and let his eyes wander along the near shore, pausing to watch as a sudden gust caught the upper boughs of a massive white pine. Its trunk rest in between two of the original tin shacks used for student housing, reaching upward eighty feet or more and leaning precipitously outward across the water. Several thick strands of webbing encircled its lower portion, used as anchors for a couple hammocks stretched idly across toward a neighboring maple. They too flapped haphazardly in the steady breeze.

"There you are!" a voice shouted, startling him.

He flinched and turned his head quickly, spying a rather plump woman in baggy khaki shorts and a plain blue sweatshirt approaching from the dirt road. She ascended the small set of stairs and waved her hands in the air. "I've been trying to get in touch with you. Is your phone off?"

He leaned forward and reached into his pocket, withdrew his cell and squinted intently at its surface.

"Well?" the woman said impatiently.

"Can't see it very well, Peg. Give me a second, will you?"

"What do you mean you can't –" she began then cut herself short when she realized his predicament. "Stop squinting, and give me that thing."

Rick handed it casually to her. "My glasses are inside the cottage, if you want to get those for me too."

"You only have one bar!" she said almost accusingly.

"Not surprised with this wind and the trees blowing all around." He reached for the phone. "What's so urgent you had to toddle all the way over here?"

Peg's breath condensed in small clouds in the cool morning air, backlit from the patches of sunlight that somehow penetrated through the forest behind her. "Do you know where Harold is? We have a critter problem."

He smirked, wondering if 'we' really meant something else. "I thought your Cabin Guide was supposed to cover all the usual suspects."

She glared at him and waved her hand theatrically about the porch. "You'll have to excuse me, your Majesty. I'm guessing you didn't hear the racket last night from your secluded palace here on the edge of campus. It wasn't a case of spiders or chipmunks in someone's cabin."

He ignored her barb about his living privilege, taking note of the dark circles under her eyes as she waited impatiently for his reply. "What sort of racket?"

Her expression softened slightly. "There were two big noises, to be more specific. And I'm not sure which one irritated me more than the other." She shuffled to the wooden bench that encircled the porch and sat down slowly. Rick was familiar with his Administration Coordinator well enough to know not to kid her beyond a certain point. The expression, 'don't poke the bear,' came to mind. Peg sighed, shook her head slightly, and then let out a throaty chuckle. "Damn students came pounding on my door at an unholy hour screaming bloody murder about a banshee underneath their cabin."

"Ah," Rick said, smiling slightly. "It's a little late for mating season, isn't it? Am I right, aren't I?"

Peg laughed again. "I can't believe you didn't hear it, even way down here. Woke up half the campus. Most were too freaked out to venture down to the source."

"How'd they get underneath –"

"Busted open an old screen covering the foundation access. The second cabin from the end on the upper road."

"Who's living there?"

"Molly Billingsley and Petra Sudol."

Rick couldn't help but chuckle. "Molly's was in my Bryophyte class this past session. I don't know Petra. Must have scared the hell out of them."

Peg suddenly burst out laughing. " I know it's mean," she said, wiping away tears from her eyes. "But, I thought the same thing. They were both sleeping completely unaware, when Molly first heard a shuffling noise below the floorboards. Then, all hell broke loose as the amorous couple started into screaming." She started to giggle again. "You should have heard those two students banging and yelling at my door saying a demon was underneath their floor."

"What'd you do?"

"What do you think? I went back with them to the cabin. I still can't believe you didn't hear it. It sounded like someone was yanking a cat's tail straight off." She gestured with her right hand as if she held a flashlight in front of her. "Shined my light into the screen. Wouldn't you know those delinquents shut up immediately and looked at me with two sets of beady eyes."

"Did they come out on their own?"

She nodded. "I backed up a little and kept my light on the hole. One of them growled a bit then popped out and scuttled into the woods as quick I've seen a raccoon move. The other came shortly after, slinking away a little more dignified."

"Did the girls go back to sleep?"

"They eventually went back in their cabin, but I doubt they slept much, if at all."

"Those coons will probably return tonight."

"Why do you think I'm here?"

Rick cocked his head slightly, wondering if it was safe to poke the bear. "I think you want me to tell you how brave you were, facing down the devil banshees."

Peg's eyes narrowed. "I'm going to ignore that, Dr. Parsons." She fixed him with a scowl they both knew was less than authentic. "Or, would it be better if I call you -"

"No," he interrupted. Rick disliked being called by his formal name, Erasmus. Hearing it always reminded him of the teasing he'd received during his formative years, despite his parents' insistence that it was unique being named after a historic botanist. "There's no need to get testy, Peg," he said casually. "I can tell you didn't get much sleep last night, and evidently you didn't come over here to get picked on either." He grinned at her disarmingly then downed the last of his coffee in several gulps. "Harold said something to me yesterday about repairing the roof over West Sparrow. I think he was planning on going up on it this morning to see if he could find out what's wrong." Rick used his thumb to point toward a cinder block building a hundred yards inland. "You might check at maintenance first, in case he's there." He then squinted at his wristwatch. "Tell you what, I'll go with you, if you don't mind. I'm supposed to meet Heather at the Ecology classroom in a half hour anyway."

Peg's eyebrows rose slightly. "And here I half expected her to come shuffling out the sliding door with a cup of coffee any second to join us."

"Heather? She's been up for a couple hours already."

"And I bet the two of you have already gone jogging together or swum the entire length of the lake or something else no sane person would do before the crack of dawn, if ever!"

"As a matter of fact – "

Peg held her hand up as she leaned forward to stand. "Never mind. I'm sorry I asked. You two are obviously made for each other."

#

The Sparrow building was like most of the older structures within the Camp, decidedly utilitarian. It had the appearance of several storage containers that had been placed end to end, creating a long and narrow space, faced on its exterior in brown metal siding and punctuated every dozen feet with equally spartan double windows. A sloping tin roof covered the entire building, including an extension midway along its length to make a simple protective porch for the two main access doors. An engraved wood sign was affixed to the outer porch wall in front of each door. The one on the left read East Sparrow, while the one on the right indicated west. A small set of worn cement steps led from the porch down to the gravel road that fronted the building, where Rick and Peg stood and peered upward at an older man sprawled precariously near the roofline above on the western edge.

Rick pointed to a spot near the sloping hillside behind the building, where the forest rose sharply with several large trees reaching outward over the roof. "It almost looks like that one could go at any time, too." It took Peg a moment to realize his meaning. He gestured to an arching trunk of a paper birch that leaned across the expanse.

"The one that came down last week was next to it," Peg said, using her hands to approximate the size of the trunk. "Must have been twenty inches. If you go around behind the Sparrow to the right, you can see where it cracked lower down. The upper part came down pretty hard on the roof."

Rick looked up again at the man. "I'm afraid to call out to him."

Peg snorted slightly and made a knowing grimace. "He can barely hear anyway, but I'd hate to take a chance you'd startle him off the roof and kill our only reliable maintenance man." She bent down and grabbed several small stones from the gravel road. "Let me handle this."

"You're going to throw rocks at him?" Rick blurted disbelievingly.

"Only near him," she admonished, letting a few larger stones sift through her spread fingers and fall to the ground. "I just want to get his attention. I'm not going to pelt him, if that's what you think." She let them fly in a gentle arch and watched as they rained down several feet from the apex, making a *rat-a-tat-tat* staccato on the tin roof.

Rick winced with the noise, convinced their handyman would jerk upward and come flailing down the slope. Instead, the elderly man lifted his head slowly and peered quizzically about, finally catching sight of the pair below.

"I need to talk to you about a critter problem," Peg shouted when she had his attention.

The man's deeply lined forehead bunched together underneath the brim of what was an equally aged baseball cap. "How's that?" he bellowed in a raspy voice, repositioning himself so that he could free a hand to cup it next to his right ear. In doing so, he lost his grip on a metal caulk gun, and it came sliding down the expanse, dropping finally with a singular thud upon the ground.

Peg tried again in a louder voice. "I said, raccoon!"

The man cocked his head. "What about it? Engine bad? One was running kind of rough last week."

Peg looked to Rick for help.

"He thinks you're asking about the pontoon." He pointed to himself and then up to where the man remained studying them with a perplexed expression. "I'll come up," he mouthed.

Harold understood this exchange well enough.

"Don't want you coming up here with me," he replied, already trying to maneuver across the ridgeline toward the waiting ladder near the far edge.

The pair watched as he gingerly backed himself over the edge and disappeared from sight.

Peg sighed audibly.

"What?" Rick asked as they waited for the handyman to descend and join them.

"Don't get me wrong," she replied bluntly. "I love Harold and all, and I know he's practically an institution here, but there are days when I wish we could have a little more efficiency with the maintenance. I have to pester him more than you know about the punch list of things that need repair."

Rick laughed. "Well, I'm glad the job of keeping him on task falls on you and not me."

"And why is that?" Her voice had a slight edge.

"Because Harold likely wouldn't listen to me as well as he does you. I suspect he's a little afraid of you, Peg. Me? Not so much. He still remembers me as a little boy running around on the north shore. And I still think of him from a boy's point of view – as a backwoods handyman who's always been a part of the lake."

"That's not what I meant," Peg said flatly. "I meant –"

"I know what you meant. You want to know why the Station Director has skirted this responsibility."

"Exactly." She glanced up as Harold came slowly around the building's corner and approached them.

"It's the sign of a good leader," he replied innocently. "I'm good at delegating all sorts of –"

"Pffft. Don't give me that –" she interrupted but was cut short as Rick gave the approaching man a friendly wave.

Harold paused briefly to pick up the fallen caulk

gun and then walked the remaining dozen yards in their direction. "Morning, Peg."

"Harold."

He extended an arm in Rick's direction. A rather meaty and age-worn hand protruded from a dirty and frayed flannel shirt. "Erasmus."

Rick didn't dare correct him. "Morning, Mr. Brill."

"What's this about the pontoon?"

"Raccoon," Peg corrected. "We've got a raccoon problem in one of the cabins."

The confusion that registered on his face from before vanished. "Which one?"

Peg pointed down the gravel road. "Second cabin from the end here on the upper road."

"Did it break through the screen?"

"Yes. There were two of them actually. Decided to use the foundation space for their own mating escape."

The older man's face broke into a wrinkled grin. "I imagine that was like a sack of cats."

"That's putting it rather mildly."

"And I suppose it'll need fixing shortly." He noticed Peg about to reply and quickly cut her off. "I should be done recaulking the leak soon enough, and then I'll get some chicken wire from the maintenance building."

Rick glanced again to the roof above. "Leak?"

"Aye – ya," he said softly. "That tree came down last week bent the hell out of the tin sheathing and tore a couple holes. I knew about the tree, of course, but not the holes." He looked back and forth between them. "Was that one staff member of yours I don't like who came hounding me. Told me to drop everything and –"

Peg's eyes widened slightly. "Oh for the love of

God. I'm sorry, Harold. He can be a bit of a pain in the –"

It finally dawned on Rick. "Peter's teaching a lab section in the West Sparrow, isn't he?"

"And I can just imagine how that prima donna got fussy about a little water leaking." She turned to the older man. "I'm sorry he –"

"Doesn't really bother me that much," Harold replied. "I've been around enough to know it's just easier to take care of something like that sooner rather than later."

"Well, I hate to add to your emergency list, but I really do need you to make that foundation repair a priority."

"Understood. I suspect no one got much sleep when those two were carrying on."

"No one but Erasmus here," Peg said casually, letting her eyes shift dramatically in Rick's direction.

Her meaning was lost on the elder man. "And then you said something the other day about the Gates' Hall?"

"About the lights. A couple more of the stage lights have burned out, and I need you to figure out a way to get up there and replace them. Plus, there's something wrong with the AV interface, but I'll have one of the students I know who's tech savvy take a look."

Harold absently swatted a mosquito that had landed on his forearm. "When do you need this?"

"In the next couple of days, if you can. We need the auditorium next Friday for the first of the guest lectures. You're taking care of the schedule, aren't you Rick? You and Heather?"

Standing there in the presence of the man he'd known most of his life and from the authoritative demeanor Peg assumed, Rick strangely felt like he was a young boy again, being told what to do. "We're working on the schedule. You can join us at the Ecology Lab in just a bit, and we'll tell you about a possibility."

Harold chuckled again. "I'll get to those coons as soon as I finish the leak. It's easy enough to see who's running the show around here, and I might as well get my ducks in order." He lifted the caulk gun and waggled it slowly back and forth as a show of goodbye. "Let me know if there's anything else, Peg." He nodded to Rick with a slight smirk as he backed away. "Erasmus."

#

The Ecology Lab was located a couple hundred yards down the gravel road from Sparrow, nestled within the trees among a cluster of similar looking tin sheathed rectangular buildings. Rick imagined this section of Camp as a small army barracks in the woods, complete with dedicated structures that served as latrines and showering facilities for the male and female students, most of whom lived two to a cabin in the nearby rows of tin shacks along the upper road.

Heather was bent over one of the preparation tables along the near wall with her back to the front door. She wore headphones and was distractedly singing an old Joni Mitchell song as the pair came through the screen door.

Rick didn't want to startle her.

Peg was enjoying the moment. She gave him a look of "you're attracted to this woman?" as Heather's Irish lilt droned on completely unaware.

"*Don't it always seem to go, you don't know what you've got –*" She stopped suddenly, sensing she wasn't alone and jolting at the sight of them. "You scared the wits out of me!"

"Hello there, Heather," Peg beamed impishly.

"Don't quit on our account."

"You could have at least given me a warning."

Rick brushed past Peg and walked over to the prep table, intrigued by the small colored mounds that sat next to one another on the aluminum surface. "You doing home economics today?"

Heather tilted her head slightly. "Did you both come here to scare and make fun of me, or was there something else?"

Peg joined them and bent down close to a red mound and gave it several sniffs. "This smells like dough." She shifted over to an adjacent bright green mound and repeated her inspection.

"It is dough," Heather replied. "I've got one more mound to mix with some yellow food coloring to complete the set. That reminds me!" She looked pointedly at Peg. "I'm glad you're here. I went jogging this morning up toward East point."

Peg cast a knowing glance at Rick and just shook her head slightly.

"That wind storm a couple days ago knocked a big branch off a cedar, and it crashed down on the feeding platform I want to use for this lab."

No one would ever accuse Peg of being slow on the uptake. "And, you want me to speak to Harold, is that it?"

Heather looked to Rick for support. "I ... er ... we ... thought you were the person to coordinate the maintenance tasks."

"Ha!"

Rick cast his eyes upward in a theatrical display of 'here it comes.'

Peg faced him directly. "What did I say earlier about being made for each other? Seems you both have no problem delegating what should be the Director's responsibility on to poor old me."

Heather glanced back and forth between the pair, trying to understand the hidden meaning.

"I'll explain it to you later," Rick said, doing his best to ignore his Coordinator's point. "How bad is it?"

Heather made a motion with her arm much like a large tree falling over. "It hit squarely on the platform and damaged the roof and one whole side. It'll need to have both repaired for it to be useable."

Peg looked again at the colored mounds. "For your cooking class?"

"A mimicry lab. I'm hoping to get it started later this week with the new session, which is why I'm doing the prep now on making the worms."

"There's another platform off the Grapevine Trail," Rick offered.

Heather nodded. "After I saw what had happened to the one at East Point, I went over to check the platform at Grapevine before coming here. It's perfectly fine, though the platform itself doesn't look like it's been used in some time."

"Probably not since Kathryn taught the Ecology class," Rick mused and looked at Peg. "How long since Kathryn?"

Peg's forehead bunched in recollection. "At least five years, maybe more."

"So, you're probably the first faculty member to use the feeding platforms since then," Rick said.

Peg sighed audibly. "You need them this week?"

Heather nodded again. "We could just get by with the one on Grapevine, but it would be better to have the East Point platform fixed so we could do some comparisons with the experiment."

"Then, as the default maintenance manager – " she looked quickly at Rick. "I want a raise, by the way," then returned her attention to Heather. "I'll go find Harold and get him to make it a priority."

Rick became suspicious. "That was too easy," he said dubiously.

"Not at all," Peg replied innocently. "Oh," she added in a tone with an obvious double meaning. "I know you both wanted to talk about the guest lecture series. You said something to me earlier about a local from Good Hart you want to include?"

Rick's voice remained even. "Yes."

"Not a problem. Just send me the information, and I'll get it posted on the web page, and I'll contact the Douglas Lake Improvement Association to let them know about the new addition."

"Just like that?" Rick said incredulously. "No fuss?"

"Now Rick," Peg added with a mock show of hurt. "I am evidently capable of doing *so many things* around this place, and I'm just thankful for the trust and authority you place in me." She turned evenly to Heather. "And you too, of course."

Rick couldn't stand it any longer. "Ok, out with it. What's the catch?"

"Well, there is one thing I need."

The pair sensed a trap had sprung.

"Go on."

Peg's mouth formed into an impish grin. "Seems none of the faculty I've spoken with are willing to volunteer this year, and I think it's important to have at least one or two participate with the students. You know how much they love it."

Rick had no doubt what she meant. Though the Station was foremost a high-caliber academic research institution, in many ways it operated much like an old fashioned summer camp, with planned events and recreational activities to help the students and faculty bond during their seasonal stay. There were dances and movie nights, athletic events and planned excursions to recreational sights throughout the upper northern peninsula. There was also, as Rick understood her meaning all too well, an annual talent show, where the students and faculty were encouraged to participate. "You've got to be kidding."

Peg pretended she didn't hear him. "I'm starting to think Harold would listen to you much better than he would to me. I mean, he technically is a direct report the Station Direction, isn't he?"

Heather finally understood her meaning. "You want us to participate in the talent show?"

"Yep," she said simply as she began backing away across the room toward the screen door.

"And do what?" Heather added in a voice an octave higher than before.

Peg shrugged her shoulders. "I've heard Rick sing before when he didn't think anyone was around." She saw him open his mouth to reply. "Don't try to deny it."

"You've got to be kidding," he said evenly.

Peg smiled and eased backward through the door, letting it close with a bang against the frame. "You've got a couple weeks to practice. I sense a Joni Mitchell duo in the making." Her voice faded as she descended the connecting trail toward the Administration Building. "It'll either be inspiring, or we'll all have a good laugh. Either way."

Chapter 5

Jack tugged his baseball cap lower and tilted his head down slightly as left Main Street and walked briskly up Bay Road toward Zoll Park a half mile ahead. He had considered taking one of the side roads to avoid having to go past the boat showrooms but decided it was riskier being recognized by one of Veronica's connections through town than from the likelihood that any employee would happen to glance street side as he passed by. As it was, the road had very little traffic this time of day, apart from the occasional seasonal resident, inbound toward town from one of their summer mansions along Wequetonsing or from farther beyond. They pedaled past intermittently, astride reproduction bicycles fashioned after a bygone era, exuding an air of confident privilege as they passed by oblivious to his presence.

He spotted her black truck tucked against a hedgerow of boxwood bordering the dirt parking lot next to the grassy expanse of Zoll Park. Jack took another glance around to make sure no one had seen him approach and walked the remaining distance. A slender woman with blonde hair stood next to the tailgate and regarded him with a neutral expression.

"Where have you been?" she said, one hand reaching into the front pocket of her khaki shorts and extracting a cell phone. She glanced quickly at the screen and then to his face.

His eyes lingered too long on her movements, appraising the flattering way the shorts exposed her shapely and deeply tanned legs.

"See something you like?" she baited, waiting for his eyes to meet her own.

"Look, Ellen – "

She had hoped he wanted to meet for a different reason. "I've taken on Kirby as forecrew for the regatta," she deflected, letting her gaze shift from his face to the harbor view several hundred yards downhill. A dozen boats sat idly at their moorings, their skeletal masts reaching upward toward the overcast sky.

Jack waited until her eyes turned back to his own. "He's got more experience on the NMs than he does in a J boat. You sure you want him running the – "

"I'll still have Steve call tactics up front. Kerryanne will take the mainsail." She took a step closer to him so that they were only a foot apart. "Of course, I could always move Steve to fore instead of taking Kirby and let you run tactics, if you want." Her lips formed into a slight playful expression. "That is, if you have nothing better to do."

Jack felt his head swim.

"But then," she added in a throaty tone, "I suppose it would be difficult to explain to your patron why you'd prefer being under me rather than running your own show."

The double entendre wasn't lost on him. "My patron, as you put it, has made it perfectly clear that I am no longer to associate with you, either under or over."

Her playful expression quickly faded. "Or else?"

"Or else, she'll leave me with nothing. I'd most certainly lose the boats, my house, and everything else."

"You could always come live with me." When he

didn't respond, she added hopefully, "Irwin would still sponsor you. You could skipper one of their Js."

He huffed bitterly. "Do you really think Irwin would continue to support me given Veronica's family connections? Trust me, I'd be cast aside without hesitation."

She took another step closer until her face was only several inches from his own. "I guess there is much to lose," she whispered. "Wouldn't you rather figure out a way to keep things just as they are?"

He studied her wordlessly for several seconds, nearly giving in to temptation. "I can't keep things the way they've been." He took a step backward. "She knows."

The playful smile slowly vanished. "Of course, she knows, Jack. Either that, or your wife is as clueless as she is –"

"She knows about the money."

Ellen stared blankly at him with the realization. "About the money," she repeated absently.

"She had someone go through our records. She confronted me with the discrepancies. There was no way I could explain where it all went."

Ellen's head jerked upward. "You told her?"

He exhaled a defeated breath. "I didn't have to. It was plain enough the money was going to you."

"And what exactly does she want?"

"It's over, Ellen." He took another step backward.

A look of fear crossed her face. "What do you mean it's over?"

"Exactly what you think. She threatened me with divorce if I continued to have any contact with you. I'd lose everything that's important to me."

She studied his face to see if there was any sign

of regret. "Excepting us, don't you mean? I don't think it'll be that easy for you, Jack. You and I are two sides of the same coin. It's no secret you married Veronica Cabot for the advantages her money's given you. I would have done the same."

"You have done the same, indirectly."

"You bastard," she whispered softly. "You know damn well you mean more to me than just the money. You always have." Her tone softened. "You and I have a history together you can't cast away so easily."

They both remained silent for several seconds. "I've always cared for you Ellen, ever since those summers on Douglas. But, like you said, we're two sides of the same coin, and I've always known that too. We'll both use people to get whatever we want. You've done the same, and now we're both going to pay for it."

"Pay for it? You'll be just fine! What about me? What will I do?"

"Go back to what you did before, I guess."

"You see me waiting tables and working retail again? You think that's going to pay for my mortgage, the bills, the boat."

Jack shrugged. "You could always sell the boat." He regretted that instantly when he saw her eyes widen.

"And then what, crew for you as a consolation? I'll get rid of my house before the boat," she said bitterly.

"That wouldn't work."

"Which part, selling the house or crewing for you?"

He knew better than to say anything.

Her reply was more an accusation. "We both know I'm the better sailor anyway." Jack glanced toward the harbor. "Irwin knows it, the yacht club, most of the other crew. Look at me, Jack."

He turned back to her. "Your point?"

"It's been so easy for you, the darling of the racing scene, with your connections and your money. Don't you dare tell me how I might manage without-"

"Like I said, Ellen. We're both cut from the same cloth, and I'm not about to jeopardize my lifestyle, despite how I may feel about you." He took another tentative step backward and glanced over his shoulder toward the road into town.

"Then you had better get going, Jack. I can see that leash tight around your collar. Go back to your pathetic wife and think of me, will you?"

He opened his mouth to say something but changed his mind and turned silently toward town.

"Better look over your shoulder now and again, Jack," she said plaintively as he walked away.

Chapter 6

Rick glanced at his watch, did a quick scan of the attendees and then signaled to one of the students near the rear. As the lights began to dim, he addressed the assembled crowd of roughly sixty people. "I'd like to welcome you to another one of our summer seminar series here in the Gates' Hall." He stood on a raised wooden stage behind a traditional podium, with a large white screen behind him containing a projected image of a magnified deep blue flower in the foreground amid an indistinct background of green roadside foliage. The title above the image, set apart within a highlighted frame read, *Foraging Douglas Lake: Various Medicinal and Edible Plants*. Beside him was a square card table, covered in white linen that draped nearly to the stage. It contained numerous specimens of plants, which Bethany Poneshing had collected earlier that day in anticipation of her talk.

He motioned to two elderly women seated in the front row. "I'd like to give a special thanks to our main stewards from the Douglas Lake Improvement Association, Allison Markle and Sue Lions, who put the word out to our lake friends about the change in our usual seminar schedule."

"Don't forget Peg!" Allison proclaimed with a slight smirk on her face.

Rick chuckled softly and turned his face to where Peg stood along the sidewall closer to the rear. She bore an expression that feigned innocence, but he knew too well she loved to complain about her perceived lack of appreciation. He extended an outstretched hand in her direction. "Of course, I'd like to thank our Administrative Coordinator, *Margaret* Kurz, for her help in organizing everything this evening." He noted with satisfaction the withering look Peg gave him with the use of her proper name.

"You're welcome, *Erasmus*," she muttered just loud enough to be heard, and this elicited more snickers.

He then turned to his right and nodded toward the woman who stood waiting on the far side of the stage. "The Biological Station is pleased to welcome our guest speaker for this evening, Ms. Bethany Poneshing."

Beth smiled slightly and tilted her head.

Rick readdressed the crowd. "I believe some of you are familiar with Ms. Poneshing's culinary skills through her restaurant called the Good Earth located in Good Hart."

One of the female graduate students near uttered a drawn out "Yummy," which caused everyone to laugh.

"She has notable experience cooking with plants that she's gathered from foraging in and around the Upper Lower Peninsula, and she would like to share with us this evening some of the commonly found species we have here near Douglas Lake." He stepped away from the podium and motioned for Beth to join him. "Let's give a warm welcome to Ms. Bethany Poneshing."

All eyes watched as Beth walked across the stage and approached the center. She wore a long, pleated skirt and a white blouse, with her dark hair pulled loosely back in a ponytail. Rick wondered if Peg had told her that most academic talks tended toward the informal side, particularly those given in the relative rustic surroundings of the Bug Camp. She waved thanks to the audience and leaned into the microphone, turning her head slightly in Rick's direction as he departed down the short set of stairs to the side. "Thank you for the invitation and the warm welcome, Dr. Parsons."

Rick skirted around the right side and took up an empty seat next to Heather.

"Please forgive me if I seem a little nervous. I'm used to speaking to audiences that are often inexperienced in biology, and in many cases the participants don't, how should I put this, do much *active* exploring in the outdoors." She purposefully allowed her eyes to scan the audience from one side of the room to the other. "I have a suspicion that neither of those things apply to the vast majority of you here this evening, and I am certainly aware that I am speaking to a group of passionate experts." She looked pointedly at the two women seated in front. "Dr. Parsons has assured me that the various DLIA members in the audience are equally as invested in the biology of the Douglas Lake area as are the Camp researchers."

The two women seemed genuinely flattered.

"With that in mind, I want to encourage you to ask questions throughout my talk." She gestured to the table beside her. "I spent some time this afternoon foraging in places I'm familiar around Douglas, and I have some representative samples to share with you." She then laughed, aware of the dubious expression Allison Markle gave her as she stared pointedly at her attire. "No, these certainly aren't my foraging clothes. When Peg spoke with me on the phone the other day, she told me it was an informal gathering. Trust me, an hour ago I could have stood here in my dusty, muck-covered clothes to show you what is often the result of foraging. After finishing my search," she brought her hand down from her chin in front of her body and toward her legs theatrically. "I thought it best to bring a change of clothes."

"Let me begin by sharing with you why I enjoy foraging in the first place. I have a feeling I'll be speaking with kindred spirits this evening." She reached for a small remote on top of the podium and clicked a button then turned her head to confirm the image had advanced. A photo depicted a large white church with a tall central bell tower and steeple near its front face. "Many of you will likely recognize St. Ignatius Church along the shore below Good Hart, in an area known as the Middle Village. Some of you may also recognize my last name as one of the older remaining Odawa families to have resided in the area in and around the Middle Village. Of course, it would make sense that I would tell you my interest in foraging grew from some direct influence of my family's heritage within this Native American settlement. After all, foraging, hunting, and trading were major employments of the Odawa peoples. In truth, though I acknowledge my ancestral roots in this regard, my family was likely no different than most of yours." She paused and looked at them meaningfully. "We shopped for groceries at Glen's Market in Petoskey."

Several people in the audience giggled at this.

"Certainly one thing that was influential growing up near Middle Village was a love of the outdoors and of time spent learning about the natural history of the area. As a child, I spent countless hours walking the trails within the woods around the Arbre d' Croche and along the shore beneath the bluffs that front the coast from Cross Village to the Good Hart. I learned the names of the wildflowers and the trees, the insects and the birds. I read books written by naturalists like Virginia Eifert, who wrote so poetically about the beauty of our Northern

Woods. Through all this, I was enthralled by the natural world here, so much so I went away to college to become, what I hoped, would be a teacher."

She paused and smiled privately, looking up at the audience with an expression that conveyed something didn't go according to plan. "Along the way, I had to change course, and through a series of unforeseen events, I found myself back up here living near Harbor, without a degree, and working for various restaurants in a number of capacities. I finally found I had a flare for cooking and was given a chance a few years ago that ended up transforming my life once again. I now own, as Dr. Parsons kindly mentioned, my own restaurant where I am able to combine my passions toward a way of life that is wholly satisfying."

She advanced the slide again. An identical image of the blue flower appeared on screen, this time without the title information. "It is one thing to know the name of something we may regard as common or rare. This here, by the way, is the Chicory flower, which is a common roadside weed that comes into its own this time of the summer. I imagine most of you have seen this beautiful, almost cerulean flower in clones along the dusty road. Knowledge through foraging requires that we know more than the name. It allows us to know these species as they are through history, folklore, biology, and medicine. There is beauty, and knowledge, and exploration involved. There is the surprise of the hunt, the pleasure in finding, and the wonder of transformation. There is alchemy in how we use the foraged foods, and sometimes there is danger. I hope to highlight some of these things this evening."

Heather turned to Rick and whispered, "I learned about Chicory after visiting New Orleans once."

Rick wasn't sure he heard her correctly. "What?"

he whispered back. "Did you say, New Orleans?"

She nodded and was about to add something else when she noticed the Lab Coordinator Monica, seated on Rick's other side with a reproachful expression. "Sorry," she mouthed.

"It is possible to eat the young leaves of Chicory," Beth continued, "but unlike certain weeds like Dandelions and Plantains, the Chicory's immature leaves remain bitter no matter how you prepare them. Believe me, I've tried." She leaned over and picked up a sample of the plant from the table, lifting it so that the group could see its green foliage and clusters of brilliant flowers. Attached beneath was a clump of rangy roots covered with loose soil. "The real value lies with the roots, which after they've been thoroughly dried can be ground into a suitable substitute for coffee. This blend is somewhat familiar in certain parts of the deep south."

"New Orleans," Heather whispered again, appearing slightly smug.

Rick shook his head, silently admiring another one of her unknown quirks.

Beth advanced the slide. An image of brilliant red flowers resembling fluffy poms dominated the screen. "Any guesses?"

Peg shouted, "Bee Balm?"

"Correct! This flower is both cultivated and wild, though it isn't as common as the Chicory. Still, you may find it in unexpected places. The plant is also known as Monarda or Oswego Tea, though there are slight differences among what are very similar species. Bee balm grows wonderfully in a sunny spot near the old cemetery next to Ignatius. It has ever since my childhood, and the distinctive smell of its crushed leaves always remind me of our warm summers. Its young leaves can be eaten raw, as can the decorative flowers, which are favorites of the bees for gathering nectar. It is a relative of old world mints and can be used as a tea substitute, with the added medicinal benefit of treating sore throats as it contains an antiseptic compound called thymol."

Bethany continued in this manner, projecting beautiful images of nearly two dozen plants and wildflowers and describing their culinary and medicinal uses. She spoke of Primrose and Garden Sorrel, Yellow Goat's Beard and Red Clover, Yarrow, Violets, Wild Leeks, and Duckweed.

Monica suddenly blurted an exasperated "Ugh," then blushed when she realized everyone heard.

Beth looked expectantly at her.

Rick was secretly pleased the normally prickly Laboratory Coordinator had made a public *faux pas*.

"Sorry," Monica said. "Duckweed. I can give you all the Duckweed you want. Seems like half the faculty end up working with it in one way or another. I've got many aquarium tanks full of the stuff, if you want a salad."

Beth laughed. "I'm not sure a Duckweed salad is exactly what I would have in mind. In small quantities, it can be blended in soups. The Chinese use it to treat flatulence."

This caused the crowd to laugh. "No doubt some of the faculty here have issues," Rick chimed and looked at Monica, who was thankful for his comic relief.

"I'd like to talk about some more general pharmacologic considerations with wild plants," Beth said, advancing the slide to a woodcut image of what appeared to be a woman gathering various plants within a deep forest. "We know today much of the pharmacology for what early colonial settlers came to understand through trial and error, often with unintended and rather unfortunate outcomes. The phytochemical basis of herbal properties lies in the secondary compounds produced by many families of flowering plants, including the alkaloids, glycosides and terpenes. These compounds are synthesized purposefully by the plants, as they require energy to produce, and so they are not waste byproducts but serve specific purposes."

She selected a plant from the table and held it aloft. "Milkweed contains the glycoside calactin, which affects the heart muscle. The wild mints grow nearly everywhere along the shore, and when you crush them they smell so wonderful, because they have terpenes. These are the fragrant oils, which have some antibiotic properties. In fact, medicinal mints overlap with culinary mints. Peppermint, spearmint, catmint, thyme, lavender, and lemon balm. Stomach problems can be treated with peppermint and spearmint. Catmint is good for falls and bruises. Mints also contain an essential oil called thujone, which can cause symptoms similar to epilepsy if consumed in large quantities. Wormwood, or Artemisia, contains thujone and the bitter compound absinthin. Wormwood was used to flavor the nineteenth century potent liquour, absinthe."

She advanced the slide again, and an image of Queen Anne's Lace appeared in close up view. "Earlier, I told you about the umbellifers like this Wild Carrot, which grows nearly everywhere this time of year. I use this as an example of the potential wonders *and* dangers that foraging can provide, and I'm often asked about the latter when I speak with people about gathering plants. The roots of this Queen Anne's Lace smell and taste like our domestic carrot but it is tough and woody. The plant's flower heads can be chopped and sprinkled on salads. The leaves can be made into a poultice for ulcers, and the fruits were once used as an abortive agent in women. It all seems fine, doesn't it?" She gestured innocently to the picture on the screen then advanced the slide again, revealing a flower that somewhat resembled Queen Anne's Lace. "Where one is useful, a close relative is not. This is Yarrow, and it grows alongside our Wild Carrot and Milkweed and Chicory. I wouldn't exactly call it harmful, but then again it should be treated with caution. It contains a rather potent blood clotting agent, which could certainly be problematic if ingested." She advanced again. "I mentioned Milkweed before. I actually use young Milkweed leaves in my late spring salads. However, like Pokeweed, Milkweed is potentially dangerous without special processing and cooking preparation. All parts of it contain heart-stimulating cardiac glycosides, and I must steep the leaves in at least two changes of water to reduce the toxicity."

"What's the most dangerous thing on Douglas?" interrupted a curious student near the back. All heads turned in his direction, including Peg, wondering who on Earth would have the nerve to interrupt.

"Many, if not most of the mushrooms are toxic," answered Bethany. "Some are notably disagreeable and will cause rather unpleasant ends if consumed in even the smallest quantities. However, some mushrooms are perfectly edible, even if they closely resemble those that are known to be quite deadly." She reached again to the table and grabbed a long reed with what appeared to be a brown tube on its end. "It's simply one of the dangers, that harmless plants like this Cattail can be problematic. I like to collect younger shoots of this plant and cook with them. I'll sauté them in butter and season them with soy sauce and ginger. Again, it sounds harmless, doesn't it?" Her expression sobered. "Cattail often grows in the same place where Blue Flag Irises thrive. I took this mature sample from up near Hook Point in North Fishtail earlier today, and I can tell you there were Blue Flags there too. When they are young, before the center stalks emerge, it is difficult to tell one from the other, unless you look carefully at the growing shoots. Cattail is edible, as I've already said. Blue Flag is quite poisonous."

She continued in this way for several more minutes, describing various edible plants from around the lake and their look-alike relatives, which were either notably toxic or quite deadly. Finally, she advanced to an image of large salad bowl filled with various greens and berries and flowers. "I fear I may have turned a bit gloomy there the last several minutes. I'd be lying if I said didn't want to scare you just a little. Consider it my planned disclaimer. Foraging is a wonderful way of learning about native plants and a means to supplement your own food stores with nutrient rich ingredients. It teaches you about the ecology of where various plants tend to thrive, including the appropriate stages of their lifecycles to maximize their usefulness. It's a wonderful way of connecting to the natural world, making you appreciate the hidden secrets all around us. However," she paused, allowing her expression to once again turn serious, "foraging should only be done by competent individuals. At minimum, it is critical you consult an expert if you are unsure about the identification or use of any plant you have found. In some cases, your life may very well depend on it."

#

Bethany stopped to chat briefly with several students who waited as she emerged from the Gates' Hall with Heather and Rick. The sun had dipped beneath the tree line on the western shore around the bay, casting the dusty main street along the Camp's frontage in shaded coolness. Heather tugged on Rick's sleeve and gestured across the road to where Peg conversed with Allison Markle and Sue Lions beside the square gazebo known affectionately as the Chatterbox. Rick observed curiously as Sue pointed animatedly toward a patch of indistinct tall grass closer to the water's edge. "Now what do you suppose that's about?" he asked her pointedly.

Bethany rejoined them, and together they walked over to meet the trio.

"It's a big problem!" Allison said almost accusingly to Peg. "We were hoping the Camp would join us in some sort of removal program." She glanced at Sue for confirmation.

"What we don't want is another spraying fiasco," Sue stated flatly.

"Most definitely!" agreed Allison.

The two women reminded Rick of the old Baldwin Sisters from the long ago Waltons television series. He laughed privately every time he thought of this. "What's the problem here?"

Sue reached down and grabbed a tufted purple flower head from a nearby plant and yanked it up for them to see. "This is the problem." A thought suddenly occurred to her, and she turned to Bethany. "Could you use this?"

Bethany looked closely at the scrunched flower in the woman's outstretched hand. It was a composite of purple tufts held within a light green calyx that was heavily textured. "Spotted Knapweed?"

The two women nodded hopefully. "If you can use it, come pick as much of the stuff as you want," said Allison.

"You could start over by Silver Strand, if you

84

like. It's taken over and is just about everywhere. There's enough to feed an army, probably."

Beth laughed. "I've not had that much success with Knapweed. The flowers are edible but not all that savory. I think it's mostly used for livestock as a grazing plant."

"I believe its foliage produces a toxin called cnicin," Heather added. "It inhibits the growth of other plants in the area and so is a particularly troubling invasive."

"The ladies here were sort of hoping the Bug Camp could work with the DLIA to do some controlled removals," Peg said, looking at Rick with an expression that suggested she needed help.

"Like what we did several years ago with the Purple Loosestrife," Sue added.

Rick remembered assisting with the Loosestrife removal along the Van Road. Mostly, he recalled the stiff back he had for nearly two weeks after the time spent pulling up plants in the swale on either side of the road. "I think the Knapweed is a different sort of critter altogether than the Loosestrife, ladies," he said patronizingly. "I'm fairly certain we wouldn't be able to make a difference at —"

Sue interrupted. "Well, we think something should be done!"

Rick pointed at the crushed flower. "Something will be. Things have a way of taking care of themselves in the long run. I grant you, you might not like the fact that it may take many years, but nature has a way of working it out in the end. Remember the Zebra Mussel scare?"

They both nodded.

"That's my point. It took years, and there's still a way to go, but the Zebra Mussel population has declined from the days when it nearly took over the lake. The ecosystem will end up rebalancing itself. My guess is something will come along that will either outcompete or consume the Knapweed, causing it to decline and the other species to return. It may take years, that's all."

Neither woman looked satisfied with his response. "But what about the problem now!" Sue exclaimed. "Something should be done about it *now*."

"And something will be done about it, Ladies, I assure you."

Peg looked askance at him. "You want us to get involved?"

Rick hoped his face gave an authoritative look. "Nope. What we'll do is just be patient, that's all." He turned suddenly to Beth, hoping to deflect the conversation. "I think you had a receptive audience this evening. Thank you for coming on such short notice."

"Oh, it was my pleasure," she replied. "And I hope it wasn't too much trouble switching the day on my behalf."

"No trouble at all," Peg beamed.

Rick's Baldwin Sisters said their goodbyes and retreated toward their beached pontoon boat several dozen yards down the shore.

Rick watched them back the boat off the sand and motor out into the bay and turned to Beth. "You're still doing the Taste of Harbor this weekend?"

"Yes. They close Bay Street to traffic past the main intersection and in front of the old depot. I'll have a booth there on Friday afternoon and Saturday morning, then I'm doing a little catering for the regatta dinner under the main tent next to the Pier. You should stop by the booth and sample some more of my creations."

Rick made a sour face and cast his eyes downward.

Beth looked at Peg searchingly. "Something I

said?"

"You'll have to forgive him. Dr. Parsons doesn't think all that much about the trappings of Harbor Springs."

"Let's just say I feel a little out of place among the people there."

Bethany glanced away and watched the pontoon boat receding toward Grapevine Point in the distance.

Rick suddenly felt as though he'd stepped in it. "By Harbor Springs, I meant the people in and around the main village. I didn't mean to suggest that your working there meant –"

"It's ok," she interrupted. "Believe me, I know how you feel. Imagine what it was like growing up in the Middle Village and having to go to high school down in Harbor." She shrugged to ease the tension. "A good many of my customers come from Harbor. Like it or not, I have to cater to them, which means putting up with their pretentious snobbery." Her smile suddenly faded, and she stared absently ahead toward the administration building, where a boy and girl walked hand in hand across the cement volleyball court and toward the stairway to the upper tin shacks. She spoke softly, almost in whisper. "They're only interested in what I have to sell at the moment, anyway. Next week, they'll be on to something new."

Chapter 7

Jack quickly downed the scotch and nearly dropped the highball as he returned it roughly to the linen tablecloth. He felt an instant tug at his senses and had difficulty focusing on the people seated around the table, let alone the other parties who were enjoying the pre-dinner festivities beneath the main tent. There were roughly twenty circular tables, each set elegantly to accommodate eight people, most of whom were various sailing teams and their significant others, dressed in a kaleidoscope of evening wear. Teams wore matching collared shirts and blazers, each with an embroidered logo and name of their hull emblazoned neatly as a badge of status. Their companions, the majority of whom were either wives or girlfriends, were dressed more formally in the latest designer eveningwear.

The annual Saturday dinner had been a Regatta tradition for the past twenty years, with Irwin Boat Shop having sponsored the event since its inception, giving them a perfect venue to advertise their services to what was typically a well-to-do clientele. They had erected the massive tent on the large common in front of the Pier restaurant Friday morning and spent the better part of the next twenty-four hours working with vendors and the entertainment to ensure a memorable event.

The weekend coincided with the Annual Taste of Harbor festival, which began years ago as a collection of small booths on the park fronting the old depot along

Bay Street. Local chefs and bakers could advertise their skills, selling their creations to an eager public, many of whom came from miles away to visit the picturesque town, to see the historic mansions and enjoy the street fair. It had grown significantly with the passing years, now including local artisans and craftsman alongside the culinary delights, with over fifty unique booths spilling out from park down along Bay Street itself, closed to traffic to accommodate the expansion.

Saturday was the highlight, as visitors could spend the morning watching the sailboats depart the harbor toward the races out in Little Traverse before taking in the vendors along the street fair or walking up along Main Street to view the historic shops and buildings. Many stayed the whole day through, waiting for the boats to return mid afternoon and then milling about the waterfront until evening arrived, with the large tent and main pier decorated festively with strung twinkle lights and live music entertaining the guests within and beyond.

Jack forcefully blinked several times, trying to clear his head. Directly across from him sat his tactician, Spencer Abernathy, whose attention was fixed several tables away toward the main stage.

"She sure as hell matched our ass both races out there," he slurred slightly, turning back to his party with an impish grin. "Had a tough time shaking her, wouldn't you say Jack?"

Jack sensed Veronica stiffen slightly to his left. "And this is why I detest coming to these things," she said acidly to him then lifted her head and fixed her gaze across the table. "Why don't you sober up, Spencer."

The others seated around them chose to ignore this exchange.

"Maybe you should loosen up, Ronnie," he

blurted suddenly. "Might improve all sorts of things for you, wouldn't you think?"

The woman seated next to him leaned over and whispered, "That's enough."

Veronica turned abruptly to face her husband and found him staring vaguely in the direction toward where Ellen Kinnear sat laughing with those around her table. She stood suddenly.

Jack's attention returned. "Where are you going?"

"Cigarette," she said tersely then backed away slowly. "Anywhere but here."

Jack started to protest to no avail, stopping short as he watched her thread her way among the tables toward the center. "What the hell is she –" he whispered. He saw the smile on Ellen's face vanish as Veronica said something to her as she passed directly by. He jerked his head toward his teammate again. "Dammit, Spence."

Ellen turned toward Jack's table, her face unreadable. "What the f?" she mouthed at him.

Another woman at his table watched the entire exchange and finally turned toward him. "You know what your problem is Jack?"

He turned to her and blinked again.

"The only good person in your life hates you, because you're a user, and the people you think are friends have been doing the same thing to you all along."

"Why don't you mind your own business, Alison," he sputtered.

"Take a look around you, Jack," she continued, emboldened by the fact no one else at the table offered any protest. "Tell me I'm not right."

He reached next to him and grabbed Veronica's half empty glass of white wine and proceeded to gulp it down. "What you are Alison, is a little bit of –"

A man in a tailored suit leaned into the microphone on the small raised stage nearest the side facing the water. A group of wait staff began to ferry dinner plates from a holding area behind the stage, placing items in front of each attendee with efficiency. "I'd like to say a few words to those of you here this evening." Conversations slowly diminished. "My name is Peter Albright, owner of Irwin Boat Shop, and on behalf of the Village of Harbor Springs, I'd like to welcome you once again to the Little Traverse Regatta." A round of applause ensued. He gestured to three people standing over toward the side who were dressed in traditional chef's aprons. "We've invited several area chefs to provide this evening's dinner selections, and I'd like to take this opportunity to introduce them. On the far left is Antoine Maison from the Placard Restaurant here in town. His staff has prepared a main course of seared Whitefish, sautéed in garlic butter. To his left we have Ms. Bethany Poneshing, owner and Chef of the Good Earth Restaurant located in Good Hart. Ms. Poneshing has made a salad using locally gathered greens and berries, complimented with bread rolls made from of recipe of her own design using acorn flower.

Jack's head came up and turned toward the front. He blinked again and stared intently, glancing away just as quickly when he found Bethany Poneshing's eyes fixed upon him. "Holy shit," he muttered softly.

"What's that, Jack?" said Alison.

"Nothing," he stammered.

"Finally, we have Ms. Tracy Cirniak of the Edible Creations in Oden, who has provided your desert for this evening. I believe our chefs will circulate around the room to introduce themselves and answer any questions you may have about their respective businesses, which I trust you will all support." More applause. "As a tradition, I'd like to announce the current standings for the lead boats following the two races earlier today." Several muted cheers ensued. "Would all team members please stand and be recognized when I call your boat name. In third place is the *Dependent*, skippered by Harbor's own Ellen Kinnear."

Jack didn't bother to glance over as Ellen stood and motioned for her three crew members to do the same. She smiled winningly amid another chorus of applause and waved briefly to the remaining guests.

"You're safe to look," Spencer said drily.

"Shut the hell up," Jack muttered, turning his head instead toward the front and finding Bethany Poneshing still regarding him coolly.

"In second place, we have the *Ambrosia*, skippered by Terry Iverson." Another round of applause as a team of four men on the opposite side of the tent rose as one and waved perfunctorily to the crowd.

"And finally, in first place is Harbor's own Jack Stinson in the *Dependable*."

"Hah!" blurted Alison, thankfully muted amid another round of applause.

Jack glared at her as he and the three companions rose. Spencer nearly tumbled over as he backed his chair away to stand.

"So there you have it, ladies and gentlemen," the emcee said. "Tomorrow should prove to be an excellent day of competition with three races run back-to-back." He gestured to one side of the tent, where several young people in black pants and white button down shirts had just finished distributing the dinners. "I'd like to acknowledge our wait staff and thank them for their assistance this evening. I'd also like to ask our drink servers to begin their rotations again. To the racers and their guests, please enjoy the evening, and try not to overdue it too much. We'd hate to see you miss the start line, because of the festivities tonight. Thanks much, and enjoy."

Veronica appeared silently beside him and took her seat, broadcasting a stale smell of cigarette smoke to the immediate vicinity. She turned to him and spoke in forced tones. "I warned you that if you so as much looked at her—"

"I know, Veronica." He looked up to see Spencer amused by their muted exchange.

A woman's voice laughed playfully as she approached, her fingers grazing the back of Veronica's neck before coming to rest on Jack's shoulder. Ellen placed herself partially between them, allowing her eyes to savor the food set in front of them before looking deliberately into his raised face. "I did everything possible today to stay with you, Jack," she said playfully. "One might think our boats turned this way and that as if we'd planned it all along."

Spencer let out a muffled laugh.

"How dare you!" Veronica hissed, turning her chair outwardly for a more direct view.

Ellen shifted slowly as if pretending to be unaware of the woman's presence. "How nice to see you again, Mrs. Cabbott." She smiled theatrically for the benefit of the table and looked back to Veronica with a hard expression. "Who knows, there's a good chance I may be the victor after tomorrow, don't you think?" Her face softened again, and she turned before Veronica could utter a reply. "Not too late tonight, Jack."

"You've said enough, Ellen," he clipped.

She laughed lightly and withdrew her hand from his shoulder then walked back to her table.

Jack lifted a fork and poked absently at his salad, sensing his wife's glaring eyes upon him. "I told you I ended it with her, Veronica."

She waited several seconds to make sure the others at the table were preoccupied with each other then leaned closer to him and whispered, "That bitch won't make a fool of me again, do you understand?"

He nodded once and lifted his fork, placing several green sprigs into his mouth.

A new voice interrupted minutes later. "I'd like to thank you all for your support this evening." Bethany Poneshing stood directly across the table from Jack and let her gaze take in the circumference. Her eyes fixed momentarily when she came to Veronica, and her expression altered slightly.

The woman seated next to Spencer had just finished eating a piece of the Acorn bread. "I've been to your restaurant before. It's simply wonderful!"

Beth hesitated and then turned to her. "That's very kind of you to say." She nodded to the half eaten slice of bread. "How do you like it?"

"It's very good. Perhaps a bit too nutty tasting for me. The salad, however, is quite wonderful."

She smiled and looked again across the table, letting her eyes settle on Jack's face. "I could have certainly used *your* support."

Jack closed his eyes and said nothing for several seconds.

A realization dawned on Veronica. "Oh dear God, not another one. Where is this one from?"

Beth walked slowly around the table until she stood behind them and whispered in a lower voice, "Why don't you ask your husband who I am, seeing that he refuses to even look me in the face."

Jack finally opened his eyes and turned to his wife. "I've never seen this woman before in my life," he declared flatly.

—

Bethany stared at him. "I guess I'd hoped for something more, at least an acknowledgement. It's been many years, Jack, and I've never asked for anything."

"I think you should go," Veronica said coldly.

Jack continued to stare at his wife's face as Bethany stood upright. "Benjamin," she said simply. "His name is Benjamin, in case you want to know." The pair said nothing as she excused herself and walked between several tables toward the tent's edge and outward into the night.

#

Jack stumbled backward and caught his heel on the curb, nearly falling into sidewalk. "Then I'll just sleep on the Goddamn boat!" he slurred, watching as Veronica backed out of the parking space in front of the restaurant and left him. A well-dressed couple emerged from beneath the portico and stopped short when they saw him wavering alone nearby. The woman grabbed her companion's hand and led him in the opposite direction.

He looked down the length of the wooden pier, mesmerized by the double vision of twinkling lights and indistinct hulls, which receded out into the harbor. He took a tentative step and nearly fell before regaining his balance and continued a meandering path out onto the dock, coming finally to the slip where the J was fastened securely.

His legs suddenly refused to cooperate as he tried to lift one and then the other over the railing. He blinked again several times and then stumbled, catching his shin and tripping headlong over the gunwale and into the space nearest the main blocks, nearly hitting his forehead on the raised fiberglass ridge that ran down the length of the cockpit floor. He lay there for nearly a minute, feeling his breath come in ragged spurts. Somehow, he managed to open the small access door and remove the spare spinnaker bag and other gear placed hastily into the v-birth beneath the foredeck. He stumbled again and pitched forward into the space, collapsing in a heap on the soft cushions inside, leaving his legs extended slightly out the door into the open air.

For a while, he lay there, strangely alert despite the increasing sensation he was losing control of his ability to see and move. His eyes finally fluttered, and his breathing became shallower – then sporadic, as short gasps escaped his mouth with each fading inhalation. He tried to lift his arm but couldn't. Tried to wipe the blood, which had begun to dry on his temple. Tried to pull his legs inside, but nothing responded. He felt a slight panic as he gave over to the urge to close his eyes.

Chapter 8

The screen door swung open quickly, and in rushed a petite dark haired girl. "I'm so sorry I'm late," she blurted as she hurried across the lab to the empty seat next to a young man with curly brown hair. He wore a notably faded Mountain Dew T-shirt, and Heather wondered if he'd purchased it that way or if he'd actually aged it through years of use.

Heather asked teasingly, "Late night?"

The girl cast a sideways glance at the boy, who suddenly slapped his forehead. "Oh damn," he muttered, looking upward to where Heather stood casually near the front. "I was supposed to wake up Melanie for lab this morning, and I kind of forgot."

"No alarm?"

The girl shook her head. "It never works. I sleep like the dead."

Heather laughed and scanned the faces of the other dozen students who sat staring at her in various states of alertness. "It's really not that big a deal, though I appreciate the apology, all the same. What's with you all, anyway? You look like you could all use a jolt of coffee."

A red-haired boy seated near the front took a deep breath and tried to offer an explanation. He stammered, "Rrrr Aaah Kk."

Heather knew better than to interrupt once he got going. She admired the boy's indifference to the stutter that could have easily been a liability.

"Rrr Aaah KK eee Horr Orr –"

"Rocky Horror Picture Show," said another girl, whose impatience got the better of her.

The boy nodded enthusiastically with a large grin.

"You've got to be kidding," remarked Heather. "How many of you went?" Eight hands shot up. "And this was when?"

The boy in the Mountain Dew T-shirt muttered sheepishly, "Started late. Someone found an old DVD, and we thought it'd be fun to do a midnight showing in the Community room. Bunch of people brought stuff to participate."

Heather laughed again. "I've never been myself to Rocky Horror, but I've heard about it. By participate, do you mean acted out during some of the scenes?"

The boy shrugged with an amused look. "Yep."

Heather loved this aspect of student life at the Biological Station. Its remoteness from any real semblance of civilization essentially fostered an environment where students resorted to what some might consider old-fashioned entertainment. Movie nights were a particular favorite, as were the periodic gatherings for flash light tag, kick-the-can, and all out battles of capture the flag. Even the graduate students and several of the faculty regularly participated in the fun.

"What's with the dough?" asked Melanie, pointing to four, large colorful mounds on the small stainless steel table next to Heather.

"Professor Parsons asked the other day if we were going to be doing Home Economics in our ecology lab," Heather replied. At this, several faces reacted with hopeful expressions, and she shook her head in mock defeat. "No, I told him we were going to be doing a Batesian Mimicry Lab, and we'll need the dough to use as an enticement for the predators." She turned around and grabbed a stack of stapled papers from the main lab bench near the front and proceeded to hand a copy to each student. "You'll find important details in here, particularly for those of who who'll be assigned to develop the randomized arrays we'll use for the feedings." She returned to the front. "We talked about mimicry in the general sense last class. Today, I want you to design an experiment to test whether or not certain factors impact the effectiveness of the mimic to model relationship."

"Take the Viceroy butterfly I mentioned last week. As the mimic, it has evolved to adopt wing patterns and coloration nearly identical to what ecologists refer to as the model organism, the Monarch butterfly. We're sometimes fortunate to have both species here at the lake as the summer wanes, though upper Michigan is a little west of their traditional migratory patterns. Be that as it may, they represent a classic relationship of Batesian mimicry – bird predators tend to avoid Monarch butterflies likely because they taste bad, and therefore the Viceroy takes advantage of this safety by having evolved a similar morphology. However, we can test whether or not this advantage is affected by relative ratios of the mimic to the model. Presumably, if the number of mimics like the Viceroy increases in comparison to the number of Monarchs, then the advantage of mimicry is threatened when periodic predation occurs and an occasional Viceroy is eaten."

Heather reached over to the table and hefted the large mound of yellow dough. "What we'll do is simulate a mimicry relationship by using this colored dough as potential food sources for the various birds who forage in two areas around the camp. We'll use a feeding platform out on Grapevine Point and another within the woods set back from the two-track that leads to East Point." A few students stared dubiously at the mound of dough in her hand, and Heather laughed, anticipating their confusion. "We're not simply going to plop down hunks of dough and watch how the birds react." She returned the mound to the table. "We're going to use pasta presses to extrude the dough into long, spaghetti like shapes, and we'll cut these into small half inch segments. Before we do that, we'll separate a portion of each color into another pile, and mix in a bit of quinine sulfate to make that particular dough bitter tasting, and then we'll extrude those in the same way that we'll do for the regular tasting dough."

"Half of you will work with me this morning to separate the dough, add the quinine, and extrude and cut into our prey pieces. We're going to need several hundred of these dough worms of each color for the experiment."

"It's starting to sound like home economics to me, alright," said someone on the far side. This elicited a few laughs.

"Fair enough," Heather joked. "Just don't mention this to anyone outside our group, if you don't mind." She extended her hand outward and swept meaningfully to the right side. "I'll divide us right down the middle. This half will work with me to construct the worms. The other half will work to develop the random arrays we'll need to set up the feedings. For each feeding station, we'll need to plan on putting out fresh dough worms twice a day, once early to take advantage of morning foragers and another around lunch time to capture any midday feeders. Those of you constructing arrays will find the instructions for doing so in the lab packet I just gave you, but basically the idea is that we need a system for distributing the worms for each feeding. The arrays are ten by ten grids, which will tell you where to place the various worms, keeping the same ratios of models to mimics. You six students will design our daily arrays. We'll need one for each platform feeder in the morning and another for the afternoon, and we'll run the experiment for a week. This means twenty eight total arrays."

"We just place the worms on the arrays?" asked a girl in the middle row.

"Yep. Once we get the worms created this morning, we'll put them loosely in separate Tupperware containers and store them in the fridge. Each day, you'll need to come remove the containers and place the worms on one of your premade arrays." She turned to the students on the other side. "You all can decide which of you will come pick up the completed arrays and take them to the feeding stations and who will go back a few hours later to switch out the trays and do the counts on which worms were eaten."

"We need to agree this morning which colors you want to use as mimics and models. One thing you can test is whether or not the birds have a sensitivity to one or more of the colors. We have green, red, yellow and blue dough. Typically, red is a signal color in nature, either for warning as in the case of certain distasteful beetles or as an enticement, like the color of certain berries. Green obviously provides a measure of crypsis, which is why so many small caterpillars tend toward greens and browns. Blue," she laughed. "Well, blue is just weird, I guess, as is yellow, but they'll at least let us try some color variations."

"Can we do two colors?" asked Melanie.

Heather nodded.

"Anyone against doing red and green?" she said to her classmates.

"Then the worm creators will make two batches of the green and red worms. One will be edible, and the other will contain the additive quinine for bitterness. You array creators will need to plan for both variants when designing the trays. Ideally, trays should have equal ratios of edible and bitter worms. I'll let you decide what the ratio should be, and we can adjust it midway through the week, if you want to test how the number of mimics affects the degree of predation for a particular color."

"What do you think we'll find?" asked another student in the array group.

"Depends," said Heather. "It will be interesting to see if there are differences in predation rates between the two locations. I imagine the composition of bird foragers is slightly different, as the Grapevine forest differs a little from East Point. Also, we may find differences between the morning predation and the afternoon. Once you've collected all the data, I'll refresh you on how to do some basic null hypothesis testing with statistics." A thought suddenly occurred to her. "Is anyone unfamiliar with statistical testing?" Several hands tentatively rose. "Ok, then. Let's get working this morning on creating the worms and designing the arrays, and then I'll spend some time doing a crash lesson on some stats we should plan to use."

#

An old two track follows the outline of the eastern shore, set back from water within mixed woods of conifers and hardwoods, whose cast off needles and leaves from the previous autumn litter the ground. It runs from South Fishtail Bay a half mile or so until it peters out in the boggy lowland where North Fishtail curves around upon itself. At one time over a hundred years ago, the road served as a logging trail, used by mill companies from the nearby village of Pellston to provide access into what was then a dark, old growth forest of towering pines.

At times, Rick tried to imagine the area nearly denuded of tree cover from the logging exploitations so long ago. Several old photographs clearly show the shoreline absent of the trees, giving the landscape a notably less inviting image than what it thankfully had recovered in the interim. He loved this stretch almost as much as the trails that wound in and around Grapevine Point across the bay. In the midst of summer, daylight filtered down through the thick canopy in muted shades of greens and yellow, making everything beneath calmly inviting, even on days when strong winds blew down the length of the lake and through the border woods. Here and there small mushrooms pushed through the needled floor, cast in relief against brilliant green moss that grew near large rocks or upon the raised berm between the well-worn tracks of the roadbed.

As Heather neared the house, she caught sight of Rick and Tanner emerging from the woods into the open space next to the maintenance hut. They spoke briefly and made their goodbyes, Tanner continuing up the gravel road toward the main buildings and Rick walked the remaining hundred yards to join her.

"Hey there!" He stopped short when he saw her waiting for him. "Long time, no see. How goes Julia Childs?"

"Funny," she said drily. "You and Tanner go for a nice little hike?"

"Working walk, I'll have you know. The Trustees need some more information on the potential replacement location for the new atmospheric tower."

"So I guess that's it on the site from last year?"

Rick shrugged and gestured with his hand toward the A-frame's front steps. "I suppose so. The Harrington debacle last summer put North Fishtail on the backburner." He purposefully followed several paces behind so as to admire her figure as she ascended the stairs. "I don't get tired of the view."

She reflexively looked over through the border trees toward the nearby water. Her voice showed the fatigue of a long day, and she stared longingly at the Adirondack chair in the afternoon sunshine on the porch. "I could use a little of that right now."

Rick chuckled impishly. "I was just thinking the same thing."

His meaning suddenly dawned on her. "Well, well my dear Erasmus. We've certainly come a long way in the two years of our relationship."

He laughed then and followed behind as they both made their way onto the deck.

"Is Tanner ok with the possible site?"

Rick motioned for her to take the chair as he deposited himself on the nearby bench along the porch edge. "I think so. The good news is the topography is more favorable. You know the old road that intersects midway and runs east up the ridge?"

Heather nodded.

"There's a suitable flat area near the summit where a tower base could be constructed with minimal engineering needed. Plus, the two-track from here to there makes a nice access for supplies and such. Tanner's only concern is that the prevailing winds down the lake might cause too much interference with certain types of research."

"So let the south tower be for forest canopy research and the new tower at east point be for atmospheric."

"That's what he said, so I guess that means he's comfortable with the possible site. How was your day, by the way? We stopped by to take a look at the feeding platform on our way back. It looks ready. Are you?"

"It took us longer than I though it would. We ended up making over two thousand of those little dough worms!"

"I just hope the students will love it."

Rick leaned forward to stand. "Speaking of which." He took a step toward her and bent down to kiss her forehead."

"Speaking of what? The students or loving it?"

He pulled back slightly to take in her face. "You of course. Loving it." He lingered a moment longer and then rose. "Care for a beer?" He walked over to the sliding door, leaving her sitting there in the sunshine with a mixed expression of fatigue and happiness.

A shadow cut quickly across the deck and leapt over the bench toward the needled ground cover. She glanced up with a hand shielding her eyes from the sun across the bay. Overhead, a tern arched gracefully in the breeze, searching for small perch in the shallows just off shore. It angled suddenly into the wind and hovered for an instant before folding back its wings and plunging headlong into the water with a splash. She watched it emerge a second later with something crosswise between its beak and lift almost effortlessly again into the air, turning toward shore to follow the wind as it climbed higher and vanished from sight above the trees.

She heard the sliding door rasp open. Rick stepped out and stared at her blankly, holding his cell phone loosely at his side. "What's the matter?" she said leaning forward.

"There was a message on my phone from Jan."

Jan owned the restaurant called the Brutus Camp Deli a dozen miles west of the Biological Station. It was popular with both locals and tourists, and served up some of the best pancakes and omelets anywhere within fifty miles. Jan grew up in the rural outskirts of Harbor Springs and had met Rick through a mutual acquaintance years ago when they were in their teens. She had spent many summer days as a part of the group of friends who ran around together on the lake, and they had remained in touch as the years progressed.

Rick walked over and sat down on the bench again, lifted his eyes to find Heather's and shook his head wordlessly.

"What's happened?"

"Jan left a message that Jack Stinson's dead."

Heather wasn't sure how to react, but she could see plainly enough the news had a profound impact. "I don't know what to say. Should I know him?"

He turned his face and stared out across the water. "Not really. We grew up together here. He was a couple years old than I.

She moved from the Adirondack chair over to sit next to him on the bench. "Did she say how he passed?"

Rick didn't seem to have heard her. "I hadn't seen him in a long time, years really." He looked at her again. "I mentioned him to you the other day. Remember at the Good Earth? I told you about a friend who started sailing here on Douglas and ended up racing in the big regattas?"

"If I remember, you said he lives in Harbor."

Rick nodded. "Jan said his boat was leading the Little Traverse Regatta this past weekend. They ran races

Saturday and Sunday. They found his body in the boat on Sunday morning."

"What! In the boat? What do you mean? Who found him?"

"His crew. They showed up Sunday morning to rig the boat and found him dead in the storage berth beneath the foredeck."

She reached over and clasped her hand into his. "Oh my God, that's awful. Did she say if they know –"

"Nothing. The message said for me to call her when I get the chance but that she doesn't know any of the details at this point."

Heather had enough familiarity with Jan the past couple years to know that wouldn't last. "I'm so sorry Rick. Was there family?"

"He was married to someone in Harbor. Quite a bit of money, I heard. I don't think there were any children."

"You should call her back. Find out about any arrangements."

"Yeah," he replied softly then glanced again at his phone. "Only one bar. Figures." He inhaled slowly and squeezed her hand. "I'm going to walk over to the Admin Building to see if I can get a better signal."

"Try behind on the upper road. You'll be less likely to run into someone there, and it's a little more out of the wind."

He nodded again.

"Do you want me to come with you?" she added.

"No." He rose and looked down at her with a forced smile. "I'll be ok. It's just weird, that's all. Hard to believe. I'll try the spot you suggested and see if I can get in touch with Jan."

Heather watched him as he descended the stairs and walked slowly up the gravel road toward the center of Camp.

Chapter 9

This can't be happening, he thought, spying the familiar black and white police cruiser parked in the tight space next to a white Station van. Rick slowed as he approached the small gravel driveway in the upper area beside the Administration Building. A petite, dark-haired woman in a crisp uniform stood nearby speaking softly with Peg. They both heard his boots scuffle on the gravel road as he approached.

"I tried to call you beforehand," Officer Bennett said.

Rick saw the empathy on Peg's face and knew his suspicions were correct. "Jack Stinson?"

Abigail nodded. "Is there somewhere we can talk privately, just the two of us?" Thankfully, Peg didn't raise an issue with the implication.

For a second, he considered leading her down the slope to the Chatterbox across the main road, then remembered her uniform and didn't want to draw the obvious attention. He glanced down at her cruiser. "Why not there. Did you pass any students on your way in?"

Abigail shook her head. "I don't think so."

"Well, you're here now, and I'd rather not chance having to explain the police presence if possible." He walked around the rear side and opened the passenger door.

Abigail said something indistinct to Peg and

waited until she walked around the corner out of sight before opening the driver's door and getting in next to him. She looked at him searchingly. "I'm sorry. I understand he was a friend of yours."

"From a long time ago, yes. How'd you know?"

Her eyes narrowed slightly.

"Never mind, you must have spoken with Jan." Rick suspected their mutual friend had reached out to Abigail for more information. "Why do I have a feeling Jack's death wasn't a natural thing?"

Abigail stared out the front window and observed a pair of students walking along the road below. The boy wore oversized hiking boots that scuffed dust with each step, raising small clouds that billowed about until caught by the wind. "There was no sign of trauma."

"Heart attack?" Rick had difficulty imagining someone nearly his own age dying under such circumstances. "No wait, you wouldn't be here then, would you?"

"The M.E. ordered basic toxicology tests. Gas chromatography showed the victim had unusually high levels of conium toxins in both his blood and urine samples."

Rick bristled at her use of the word victim. "Look, Abby," he said with a hint of irritation. "It's just you and me here. I'm an algae guy, remember? You mind helping me with conium?"

"It's an alkaloid toxin, similar in structure to nicotine."

"Where the hell would he –"

"Toxicology identified it as a *Conium maculatum* derivative.

He recognized *maculatum* from Bethany's talk. "Hemlock?"

"Poison hemlock. An autopsy revealed the victim still had significant stomach contents. Evidently, this correlates with conium ingestion. The M.E. said poisoning would have been quick, probably less than a couple hours. Not enough time for the stomach to empty." She looked meaningfully at him. "I need you to identify the contents."

"Jesus, Abby! How bad would it have been?"

"Tough to tell. Not as much as water hemlock, according the M.E.. I guess that's pretty horrific. Poison hemlock shuts you down while it puts you to sleep. He probably died of respiratory failure but was already unconscious."

"Where was he beforehand?"

Abigail regarded him stoically.

Rick sighed. "Right. Just like two years ago. You're not going to tell me much at all."

"You know I can't compromise the investigation. Yes, you've already collaborated with our Department before, and this lends credibility, but trust me, a DA would have a field day if we didn't follow standard protocol for your part."

He ignored her brief monologue. "Last Saturday was the Little Traverse Regatta. Isn't there some sort of dinner that takes place? Was he there?"

She placed both hands on the steering wheel in the ten and two and squeezed slightly. "You know I can't say much more."

He waited nearly a minute before speaking. "Fine. When can you have the samples here?"

"First thing in the morning."

Rick nodded. "I want Heather to assist me on this." When Abigail started to object, he interrupted. "She already knows about his death. Between the protocol and the damn paper work I know you'll need, it's going to take me an entire day. She'll figure it out, and I'd rather not make up some flimsy excuse." He glanced over through the driver's window at the Administration Building. "What about Peg? She's no fool."

"She's promised to keep quiet."

"Ha!" he said sarcastically.

Abigail looked sternly at him. "She has given her word to keep this confidential. At any rate, all she knows is that I've asked to speak with you. There's nothing risky in her connecting the dots that you'd be doing the forensic work, provided she keeps it to herself."

"What if I can help with more than the forensics?"

"Meaning?"

"We all knew Jack, for Christ's sake! Maybe there's something else I can do."

"Start with the forensics. Once you've completed your report, we'll see." Her expression softened. "I am sorry, you know."

"And why me, again?"

"Like I said, you've got a track record. Only a couple cases, but it's still important. I trust you. I know you're meticulous, and we don't exactly have another specialist in identification of this type within a hundred miles."

Rick exhaled. "Not exactly a track record I'd prefer."

#

Heather removed two small Tupperware containers from the cooler and placed them side-by-side on the Formica lab bench. "What did you say to Monica?"

"As little as possible." He reached over to a box of Nitrile gloves and removed a pair then slid the box over to her. "Told her I cancelled my lab section for the day and that my class wouldn't need the prep anymore."

"Those are medium. I need the small size." She searched around the lab and spied an open box closer to the washing sink across the room. "I bet she was a little miffed."

"A little. She let me know she'd already done an hour's worth of reagent preparation and how she didn't appreciate my wasting her time."

"She does remember you're the Station Director, doesn't she?"

"You know Monica." He glanced at the piece of paper Heather removed along with the containers. "These are Stephen's notes. His post mortem analysis of the gastric samples puts the time of death at two hours. The sample in the red Tupperware has had ten percent formalin added to denature the enzymes and kill any bacteria. It should be cold."

Heather stopped putting on the remaining glove and placed the bare palm against the side. "It's cold."

"The one in the green container didn't have the preservative added. It should be frozen."

"It is. Why the difference?"

"Formalin would start to break apart any DNA in the material. We'll use the preserved sample with the scopes today. Put the frozen container back in the cooler, and put that in the freezer for now. We'll keep it in case we need to send away for DNA analyses." He positioned the red container next to him and reached for a box of nearby microscope slides. "Let's work on making a dozen or so mounts using what we have."

Heather removed a box of fifty milliliter glass vials with screw tops from an overhead cabinet and

113

placed several on the table. "What else?"

"I stole a bottle of picric acid from Monica's stock."

Heather clicked her tongue. "Lying and stealing from Monica. Better hope she doesn't find out."

He inhaled deeply. "I guess we can get started." He paused and stared at the unopened container.

"You still haven't talked about it."

"I know."

"Afterward?"

"Yes. I just don't want to think too much about what we're about to do. It feels like Sondra all over again from two years ago."

Heather recalled the way they both had to disassociate from the stark reality that they were analyzing organ samples from a station colleague, one who was living and breathing only days beforehand. "So what do we do?"

Rick opened the Tupperware and used forceps to transfer a small quantity of what resembled a mucous-like stew carefully into one of the vials. He then added several drops of Safranin 'O' stain, let it sit for thirty minutes and then followed with a wash in the picric acid. Finally, he used the forceps again to transfer bits of material from the vial onto several of the glass slides, taking care to spread any filaments evenly so light could pass through when possible. When he'd finish one slide, Heather carefully used a pair of tweezers to place a coverslip onto the sample, using blotting paper over the top to remove any bubbles that had formed beneath.

When they had prepared a dozen slides, Rick removed his gloves. "Let's start the paperwork now while these dry. It's going to take an hour or so. You may as well put the Tupperware back in the fridge."

She tugged on his hand as they left the Lakeside Lab. "What?" Rick said.

"I know it's close to supper, but let's not go home just yet."

He turned his eyes down the length of the main gravel road. A group of several students were walking away in the direction of the dining hall in the distance. "Fine," he sighed. "I'm not really hungry, anyway. Are you?"

She shook her head. "Not after that. Maybe later. Let's go for a walk instead, ok?"

He turned his head in the other direction, spying the worn entrance gate at the edge of the forest path leading into the Grapevine Trails. "I could use some fresh air."

The single track led immediately into a stand of mixed hardwoods and skirted the western edge of the bay as it meandered nearly a third of a mile toward Grapevine Point. They ascended a slight rise and passed a small open space in the woods where Heather's feeding platform stood empty. She said nothing as they continued onward, content with sounds of the songbirds calling to one another and the wind blowing through the canopy high overhead. Further on they passed a hammock strung between two paper birch trees. A young woman was nestled inside reading an old hard cover book. She looked up when she heard their feet on the brittle leaf litter still left over on the trail from last autumn's production.

"Hey Professors." She wiggled awkwardly in an attempt to shift into a sitting position, dropping her book in the process.

Rick smiled, choosing not to correct her for the

formal title. "Hi, Emily. It's nice out here." Downslope a few dozen yards through the trees, the water lapped quietly against the shoreline. "Sorry to disturb you."

Heather bent down and retrieved the book, glancing at the title as she handed it back. "Land of the Snowshoe Hare."

"That speaker the other day mentioned the author, and so I looked her up."

Rick leaned in for a closer look. "Virginia Eifert."

The girl nodded. "Turns out they had this copy at the Cheboygan Library, so I took a chance."

"Do you like it?" Heather asked.

"She was right. It's wonderful. Reminds me of here – the descriptions, her emotions, the way she writes about living in the northern woods. It really is beautiful."

Rick absently inspected the worn webbing holding the tattered hammock in place. "Well, you've got the perfect spot for some alone time. We're going around the trails ourselves for the peace and quiet, so we'll say our goodbyes." The girl smiled and nodded wordlessly as the pair continued onward toward the point.

After several minutes, Heather said, "Anything on the news this morning?"

Rick knew she meant on the Internet. Though the Station Director did have one of the nicest faculty cottages in the Camp, in most ways it was as rustic as the rest of them without television service, though a few faculty resorted to installing their own satellites for the summer. Even that was spotty because of the tree cover. "There's not much. Jack's body was reported to have been found by two of his crew Sunday morning when they were going to prepare the boat."

"No mention of a cause of death?"

"Only that he was last seen at the Regatta dinner."

"With his wife?"

"And crew and their guests."

They walked on in silence for several more minutes. The trail turned westward slightly as it followed along where the point jutted outward into the lake then angled to the southwest through a transitional zone of conifers as it ascended a notable ridge. "Tanner told me this ridge is a left over from the glacial retreat."

He didn't expect that from her. "You and Tanner do a lot of walking out here?" he teased.

She was relieved for his playfulness. "Sometimes. When you're not around."

He laughed. "This whole area was one big glacier fifteen thousand years ago. I read that this section was near the edge of what was a large lake as the glacier began to retreat." He reached over and held her hand again. "I suspect Tanner knows more about this than I do."

"Yes, but you make it sound so academic. Look, Tanner is my forest fling, and you are my algae guy. I hope you're ok with that."

"Thanks." He squeezed her hand and smiled sarcastically.

Her expression altered slightly. "Do you feel any better?"

He inhaled deeply and looked upward at the blue sky between boughs of deep green cedars. "I do." He lowered his head and met her eyes. "Thanks for the help today."

"How soon until it makes its way into the news?"

"I couldn't say. Our report adds to the toxicology findings. I didn't have a chance yesterday to ask Abigail if there were any suspects at this point. It wouldn't have mattered anyway. She wouldn't have discussed it with me prior to our work." He scuffed his shoe absently at a clump of sere pine needles, exposing the humus beneath. "I just can't believe it. How the hell did he get poisoned?"

She said nothing for several seconds and then looked at him speculatively. "You know, there is the obvious link."

"I know," he nodded. Somewhere overhead came the shrill screech of a red tailed hawk.

"Should you tell Abigail?"

He shrugged. "Probably, but she made it fairly clear I was to stay out of the investigation."

"I feel bad even thinking it."

Rick motioned for them to continue. "So do I, but she *was* supposed to be catering the event, and it's hard to ignore the fact she'd likely have ready access to the plant. This assumes she knows him in the first place, and I feel guilty even suggesting a possible connection."

"Still no idea why anyone would want him dead?"

"No."

They walked on a little further. "What was he like?"

"I knew him when we were kids. I was maybe twelve or thirteen. He was a couple years older. His family used to come up summers at a cottage down the road from ours. I think they were from Ohio or Indiana." His face scrunched trying to remember. "Ohio. Cincinnati, I think. I remember he used to wear an old Reds baseball hat on the boat."

"You said he was a good sailor."

"Very good. I mean, we were kids, and we got to crew on several of the Lightning boats around the lake, but Jack had something special about him. He could read the water and know how to trim the sails. I envied him in a way, because he was often favored by other skippers when they needed a spare crew."

They came to a place where a large white pine had uprooted and had fallen across the trail. Bits of what looked like fresh soil still clung to the massive root ball a dozen feet off the path. "I bet this came down two nights ago in the wind storm."

Heather pictured the massive white pines that loomed over their A-frame. "I think about that every time we get a storm and those giant trees over the porch sway. If one came down on the house, we'd be —"

"Blammo," he interrupted.

"It's not funny."

His smile faded. "Nope. Sorry."

"Wait! Is his family still on the lake?"

"No. They sold the cottage many years ago. I think I was in college at the time. I saw him a few times here and there for a couple summers afterward. I think I told you he started spending more time in Harbor Springs, didn't I?"

"That's what you said the other day."

"I haven't seen him now in maybe fifteen, twenty years, but I've read about some of his races. There were a bunch of us who were part of the Lightning group. Andrew, John, Matty, Peach, Jack and Ellen. I should probably get in touch with Peach to see if she knows."

"I haven't met any of the others, have I?" She thought of the Fourth of the July party on the north shore where she was introduced to many people.

"Just Peach. The others don't make up often at all. I haven't seen Ellen since those sailing days either."

They came to the place where the trail ended at the old two-track road which ran west toward Pellston through the woods and east back toward their colleague David's research field on the bluff above the Camp. The road was notably level and straight after the curving undulation of the Grapevine trail, cutting through a section of woods where the ground was sandy. Heather let go of Rick's hand as she walked along the left track, admiring the moss-covered berm that separated them.

"I'm getting hungry," she said finally as they approached the Camp perimeter.

"Me too. What are you fixing?" He grinned at her.

"I'm fixing a bottle of red wine, if that's ok. Shouldn't take long at all. In fact, it'll probably be ready when we get back to the house."

They descended a rough paved road and came upon the spot where they'd begun their walk an hour ago at the Grapevine gate. "I needed that," Rick said simply.

"I'm sorry about today," she said affectionately. She glanced around to make sure they were alone then reached up and kissed him full on the mouth, lingering for a few seconds before pulling away.

Not far off, where the upper road made its way past the old row of student tin cabins, several students sat around a makeshift campfire. Two boys let out a catcall whistle after Heather kissed him. "Woo hoo, Professor Wilkins!" one of them shouted.

Heather turned toward them suddenly. "Oh God," she gulped. "I didn't see them! How embarrassing."

Rick laughed and waved at the trio. "Nothing to see here," he shouted, taking her hand and leading her down the middle trail toward the main gravel street below.

Chapter 10

Veronica held the intercom button as she studied the small video screen. "Yes."

"This is Officer Bennett," came the metallic reply of Abigail's voice. A loud buzz signaled the gate release, which swung slowly inward and permitted clear passage up the curving fieldstone driveway. She steered the cruiser past a private tennis court, nestled within a manicured lawn that backed up to the edge of the Lake Michigan shoreline. The drive ended in a broad circle in front of a large white house that had been the Cabbott estate for several generations in Harbor Point.

The historic homes within this private community were modest compared to the near vulgarity of contemporary mansions, competing with each other as Harbor Springs wrestled with its popularity among the nouveau riche. Abigail couldn't help but admire the clapboard "cottages" that reminded her of images of old estates on Nantucket or Long Island. Harbor Point thrust outward from the land as a peninsula beginning near the outskirts of the village center and extending outward into Little Traverse Bay. A small guardhouse stood at the neck to prevent anyone but residents from entering their private seclusion.

Abigail opened her door and exited the car as Veronica Cabbott emerged from the front doorway. "I trust the guard didn't give you any trouble," she said neutrally.

"No, though they weren't exactly helpful either." She adjusted her uniform and placed her officer's cap squarely on her head.

"The guards are paid to be suspicious of anyone outside the community, you understand. We can't afford to have tourists driving through here."

Abigail considered asking about the need for an additional security gate, but decided any answer would likely be above her pay grade. "As I mentioned to you on the phone, I'd like to speak with you again about the night of your husband's death."

Veronica nodded solemnly and stepped to one side, gesturing with her arm for Abigail to lead into the front foyer. "May I offer you some coffee, Officer Bennett? Why don't you have a seat in the adjoining parlor through there."

"Yes to coffee, thank you. Black is fine." She walked dutifully through an arched doorway into a small sitting room and waited until Veronica returned, holding a large mug in each hand.

"I don't understand why you need to speak with me again. I had hoped you were coming with information."

Abigail listened with a neutral expression. "Once again, I'd like to offer my condolences in what must be a very trying time for you and your family. I know how difficult it must have been to answer my questions so soon after learning of your husband's passing. Please understand, the investigation is in its initial phases as we do whatever we can to gather as much information as possible. I'm still waiting on the formal report from the autopsy, and I am in the process of speaking to various individuals who were known to have contact with your husband in the hours leading up to his death."

Veronica's tone rose notably. "It's been over

seventy two hours, Officer Bennett, and I have been told precious little of the nature of Jack's death."

"You must understand, Mrs. Stinson –"

"I think it's safe to assume you've ruled out a natural death."

"The county Medical Examiner has found no evidence to support death by a natural cause. All I can say now is that my investigation is proceeding as quickly as possible."

Veronica lifted the coffee cup slowly and brought it to her lips without once taking her eyes off Abigail's face. She took a cautious sip and lowered it slowly to the table between them. "Go on," she said simply.

"I'd like to go through your recollections of the regatta dinner again. I understand we spoke about this less than three days ago, however, I've often found that witnesses have more information to share when a bit of time and distance has occurred."

Veronica's eyes widened. "What do you mean by witness? Are you suggesting that I'm-"

Abigail put her hands up to stop the woman's speech. "Please don't misinterpret. Any person who had either come into contact with your husband that evening or had secondary information that could be useful in my investigation is considered a witness, that's all."

"But I didn't *witness* anything in particular!"

"I understand, ma'am. Would you mind describing the evening again."

Veronica finally broke eye contact and glanced down to inspect the folds of her pleated summer skirt, absently rolling the fabric back and forth between her thumb and forefinger. "Jack insisted on arriving late, which was fairly typical. We took my car from the house and drove down to the Pier."

"I'm surprised you were able to get –"

"Reserved. Irwin has an arrangement with the Pier to have half their lot set aside for certain attendees of the regatta dinner."

"Your husband is a VIP, I take it." Abigail then winced slightly. "Forgive me."

"Jack sailed for Irwin, you see. His notoriety was certainly something important within the sailing community."

"Would you clarify what you mean by notoriety?" Abigail thought she saw a strange expression on Veronica's face.

"He brought recognition to the sailing community through his successes, that's all."

"How many boats does he sail for Irwin?"

"All told, three. The J boat, a Melges and one of the older NMs."

"And Irwin owns all three?"

"Only the J boat. The others belong to my family."

"And when you got to the dinner?"

"The majority of the guests were already in attendance. We were the last couple to arrive at our table."

"You were familiar with everyone?"

Veronica nodded. "His sailing crew and significant others." She placed a distasteful emphasis on the latter. "I assume you've already spoken to them."

"In the process of doing so," Abigail replied noncommittally. "Their recollections have been a bit spotty, to be candid. I assume there'd been a bit of drinking?"

"And other things."

Abigail let nearly ten seconds pass in silence to see if se would offer any additional information. "I'll ask you again, do you remember anything unusual about the dinner, anything at all, no matter how insignificant it may seem?"

Veronica's expression remained flat. "The evening passed as they often do under these circumstances."

Abigail decided on a different approach. "Can you think of anyone who may have wanted to –"

"hurt my husband?" Veronica finished.

"Perhaps," Abigail said simply. "Any business dealings? Debts?"

"Not that I'm aware." She then laughed ruefully. "However, my husband's business, such that it was, was managing and spending my family money."

"What about personal matters?" The woman's face turned guarded. "I spoke with someone who led me to understand, and please forgive me for asking, your husband had difficulty with fidelity."

Veronica's expression didn't change. "I don't believe that was a question."

Abigail said nothing.

"I don't care where your questions are leading, Officer Bennett. It's been almost three days, and this is the extent of your investigation?"

"The person I spoke to described an interaction that took place at your table." Veronica's eyes turned hard. Abigail deflected. "Would you confirm that you and your husband were seeing a marriage counselor in Petoskey."

Veronica lowered the cup quickly. "I am under suspicion?"

"I'm merely conducting an initial inquiry, Mrs. Cabbott."

Veronica rose, clearing signaling the discussion was at an end. "I think I would like to speak with my lawyer at this point."

Abigail sighed, nodded and took a last sip. "This was excellent coffee, by the way." She stood and faced the host directly. "You are certainly within your right to retain counsel. One last thing, does the name Ellen Kinnear mean anything to you?"

"I believe you've just asked a question for which you already know the answer," Veronica replied coldly. She hesitated as Abigail turned and walked to the front door. "Jack's indiscretions were unfortunately not quite discreet."

"And I suspect that must have upset you terribly."

"Not to the degree you're implying." She opened the door and stood to one side. "I'll await any information you have to share."

Abigail nodded once and backed away toward the front steps.

#

The village of Pellston sits roughly four miles due west of the Biological Station, nestled at the crossroads where U.S. 31 intersects the county road leading between Douglas and Burt Lakes to the east. The town was formed during the lumber boom of the late nineteenth century, when large mill operations provided the majority of employment as tens upon thousands of trees were cut and processed for nearly forty years until the industry collapsed. Though still a going community, the village serves mostly as a stop over for tourist traffic headed either north toward the straits or south to follow the inland lakes. It's main street consists of a few hardscrabble buildings from a bygone era, an old train depot where the railway used to run, and a collection of antique stores, a gas station, a dollar store, and a diner called the Small Town Grill.

Rick waited until Abigail had settled into her chair across from him and ordered a cup of coffee. The waitress nodded soberly at her and gave Rick a curious expression as she turned to deliver a ticket to the cook, who worked busily in front of an open grill.

"Nothing to eat?" Rick asked. "I'm going to have a late breakfast."

Abigail shook her head.

"Must be in some kind of trouble," goaded the cook sarcastically, giving a sideways glance in Abigail's direction.

"Mind your business, Clive," Rick replied in a tone he hoped suggested there was no need to be nosy.

The cook chuckled, clearly pleased with himself. He grabbed a large cleaver from a wooden block and proceeded to dice a mixture of cooked potatoes and bacon.

"Clive knows me," Abigail said simply.

"Oh, I know Abby Bennett," he said playfully. "Must be official Bug Camp Business." He stopped chopping and held the cleaver in their direction. "Still working on the murder from last year?"

Rick suddenly wished he'd picked another location.

Abigail turned toward him. "Clive, it might surprise you I am here on social business." She cut him off when she saw he was about to make a caustic response. "Don't let your mind wander. This is simply a meeting about Camp affairs, which have nothing whatsoever to do with anything, especially you."

"Whatever you say, Abby," he replied still laughing. "Makes me a little nervous when the fuzz shows up at my restaurant and doesn't even have the decency to order – "

"Fine!" she relented. "An omelet then. Denver."

"Denver?" he teased. "What the hell is - "

Abigail gave him another hard look.

"One Western omelet it is. Was that so hard, Officer Bennett?"

Rick lifted a manila folder he'd kept on the bench next to him. "I was going to slide this across the table to you, but I think I'll just wait and give it to you after we leave."

Abigail huffed. "What did you find?"

"Bottom line?"

She nodded.

"There were a number of different plant cells and seed casings still identifiable in the samples. We were able to positively match spinach, carrot, dill, turnip and strawberry."

"That's it?"

"You know that's not it." Rick exhaled slowly. "There were hemlock cells."

"Seed or leaf?"

"Does it matter?"

"It might help determine how it was given to him."

Rick glanced out the picture window, where a southbound car had stopped alongside a rudimentary farm stand and an elderly couple was inspecting what looked like large zucchinis. "The only cells we found corresponded to leaf material, mostly epidermal and a few from conductive tissues. We were able to positively match from guard cells within the epidermal samples."

"I assume you've included images in the report."

"Yes, and we made sure to document the entire custody protocol. I assume you want us to hold onto the samples for the time being."

"For now," Abigail replied. "You can't do any

DNA typing, right?"

Rick shook his head. "Not with your protocol restrictions. I'd have to send out those samples downstate if you need sequencing."

The waitress returned with two large plates of food. "Blueberry cakes for you, and a Western omelet for the fuzz."

Abigail gave her a stony look.

"Clive made me say it," she replied sheepishly as she backed away.

Rick dripped syrup liberally on the pancakes and then spread a quantity of whipped butter on the side order of Texas toast. "On second thought," he slid the manila folder across, "take it. Clive doesn't really give a damn one way or another. He just wants to stir trouble."

They ate silently for several minutes, content to observe the few locals who'd wandered in for a cup of coffee or a bite to eat. Two men dressed in tattered overalls and filthy shirts seated themselves at the counter in front of the grill and proceeded to compare notes on the latest solutions to the morning's Detroit Free Press crosswords. They pulled in their stools suddenly as a pair of well-dressed women attempted to negotiate the narrow space between the counter and the booth table opposite, where they took a seat and inspected the menu.

Rick took another sip and regarded Abigail speculatively. "Now that we've finished our report −" He trailed off, seeing what he though might be a warning expression on her face. "Look, Abby, Jack was my friend at one time. I'd like to know what the hell happened to him, beyond the fact that somehow he got poison hemlock in his system."

Her face softened slightly. "Off the record −"

"What record?" he chided.

She ignored his reproach. "I interviewed his wife early this morning. Do you know her?"

Rick shook his head. "I only heard he married into money."

"That's putting it mildly. From what I've been able to piece together, Jack Stinson has certainly made the most of Veronica Cabbott's family wealth."

"Veronica *Cabbott*!"

Abigail smiled ruefully. "She made it clear to me she has always preferred Cabbott to Stinson."

"Is she a suspect?"

"Possibly. There were marriage problems. He was rumored to have several affairs. They were in counseling."

"You talked with the counselor?"

"No. Confidentiality issues. One of the dinner attendees I spoke with was a little forthcoming with information. Evidently, Mrs. Cabbott and her husband had a quarrel at the regatta dinner about his indiscretions. His alleged lover was also in attendance at another table. Apparently, there was some sort of scene. Mrs. Cabbott excused herself for several minutes prior to the table being served."

Rick's eyes narrowed. "Your suggesting she could have –"

Abigail shrugged. "She had motive and opportunity, that's all. It's thin, I grant you, but it's the primary thread at this point.

"Wait, you said his mistress was also at the dinner? She must have been a wife or girlfriend of one of the other sailors."

Abigail shook her head. "Now, we're getting into the grey area of what you need to know."

The waitress returned with a fresh pot and filled Abigail's before glancing at Rick.

He placed his palm over the half full cup. "No, thank you. I will take the check, when you have a chance."

Abigail waited until she left. "What are your thoughts about the hemlock?"

"Someone must have put it in the salad."

"Wouldn't it have looked different?"

"Not necessarily. The leaves resemble something between parsley and turnip, and it would have been relatively easy to tuck a few sprigs into the mix."

"A few?"

Rick nodded soberly. "A few small leaves would do it."

"That's the thing," she said. "Tuck them into *his* mix, not the whole bunch. The salad dishes were likely prepared beforehand separately in side bowls and then delivered to each table. This leaves two possibilities. One, the sprigs were placed during the preparation and then delivered to the table, or two, someone dropped them into his bowl once it was already on the table."

"The second is more likely. There's no way to control which salad goes where once the waiter picks up the tray. The murderer would have to know exactly which salad bowl was Jack's beforehand."

"Unless there had been a special order for him. Something unique about his bowl to ensure only he got it."

"I imagine that would be relatively easy to determine."

"I'm arranging to meet with the wait staff and the catering," she replied.

Rick debated whether or not to say anything about Bethany. He knew if he did, Abigail would probably cut him out of the investigative loop.

"What?" she said, seeing a distant look on his

face.

"There's still the issue of getting fresh hemlock in the first place," he recovered. "It's not that common up here."

"How uncommon?"

"More than it used to be. Much has been purposefully destroyed from the wild places where it's been positively identified." He looked tentatively at her. "Heather and I know someone who specializes in edible and poisonous plants around the area. I could speak with this person confidentially, if you want."

Abigail started to protest and then paused. "Confidentially?"

He tried to make his voice sound innocent. "We'll just say we're developing a brochure about invasive and dangerous species for the lake residents and need some assistance identifying potential locations."

She mulled over the suggestion for a second as the waitress returned with the bill. "Brunch is on the department. I'm headed back to Cheboygan to deliver your report to Steve."

"How long until you have to disclose to the press?"

"The coroner's office is waiting for Steve's final report before releasing the body. The press will be notified shortly thereafter. Late this afternoon, most likely. When can you talk with you plant specialist?"

"It'll have to wait until tomorrow. Heather's taken her class up to Sturgeon Bay this afternoon to do some fieldwork. I've got a meeting with the Trustees I can't reschedule. I'll set something up for first thing in the morning."

"Fine," Abigail exhaled. "I'd rather join you, but I have to be in Harbor again tomorrow morning." Her face bore a pained expression. "With the press release this evening, I'll likely have to return to Harbor Point." She lifted the bill from the table and stood. "Can you take care of the tip? I'll pay up front on our way out."

As they turned and began walking past the open counter, a group of teenagers made their way noisily into the eating area, providing a fortunate distraction for Clive, who merely watched the pair exit without making a comment.

Chapter 11

The building resembled a small log sided barn stained dark brown. It had a tin roof topped with an old cupola and a covered post and beam front porch. A small sign next to the road read "Brutus Camp Deli" in plain green letters with the hours of operation given beneath. It was a popular restaurant year round, appealing to both locals and tourists with a quality menu, ample portions and interesting décor, consisting largely of local hunting and fishing photographs, lures and trophies.

Heather lightly touched Rick's arm and gestured at an old white truck parked in the grassy area behind the restaurant. "You think that's hers?"

He slowed and turned into the gravel lot. "That's Jan's." He maneuvered behind the building and came to rest next to the truck, pointing to an overflow lot on the other side of the building hidden from the main entrance. An old Subaru was parked next to a white propane tank. "That's probably hers. It could be the cook's, but I seem to remember Jan said he only lives a quarter mile away up Brutus Road."

"They're open." As she said this, another car pulled into the gravel lot and came to a stop next to the side entrance.

"Just. I told Bethany to meet us at eight. Jan will be the only one here for the first half hour until the breakfast rush builds, and she'll be distracted enough."

"We could have just as easily met her in Good

Hart –"

"Too private. I know Jan's a risk, but she'll behave. The Deli is a perfect neutral ground, and there will be people here, just in case."

Heather muttered a soft "oh boy" as she exited the car and waited for him to walk over to the front doorway beneath the porch.

Several bells fastened above the door chimed as it swung inward. A heavyset waitress with short salt and pepper hair was busy seating the group ahead of them. She glanced upward upon hearing the bells and smiled. "Good morning, Professor Parsons."

For a moment, Rick was dumbfounded at this unconventional greeting by his life long friend. "Morning, Jan." She nodded her head meaningfully toward the far side, where a woman sat alone at a small table in the corner.

Bethany looked up at this exchange and gave a small wave.

"And to you Dr. Wilkins," Jan added.

Heather wasn't sure whether she was kidding or not but decided to play along. "Morning."

"I'll be right over after I take this table's order. I assume coffee for both of you?"

Rick glanced over to the corner table and saw Bethany already holding a cup.

"That'd be fine, thanks."

Bethany stood as they approached. "It's been a long time since I've been here," she said, reaching across the rustic wooden picnic table to shake hands. She noticed reserved expressions on both their faces. "Your voice on the phone yesterday suggested this isn't exactly a social get together."

Rick glanced nervously at Heather. "No. It's not. I apologize if I sounded a little mysterious." Rick was about to continue when Bethany interrupted.

"Let me see if I can help. The news this morning reported that the sailor who died following the Little Traverse Regatta banquet was murdered. The coroner's office disclosed the cause of death due to poisoning from the alkaloid conine, most commonly found in the plant poison hemlock." She paused and lifted the cup to her lips, waiting for their reaction. When they said nothing, she nodded slightly. "I see. It makes sense I could be a potential suspect."

Heather tried to interject. "We're not here to-"

"The news also indicated you were assisting in the investigation."

"How in the hell – " Rick started.

"Abigail Bennett was quoted as saying the Biological Station was working with the coroner's office during the investigation. The reporter commented on the relationship you've had with the Cheboygan Police the past two years."

Rick nodded. "I'm a little surprised she said anything, but I guess it doesn't matter at this point."

Bethany shoulders slumped a little. "I realize this looks bad, but I want you to know I didn't have anything to do with Jack's death."

Rick thought he heard something in the way she said his name. "You knew him," he guessed.

Bethany nodded slightly.

"The other day, at the Bug Camp, during your talk you mentioned something about a series of unforeseen events and having to return home. Then afterward, at the Chatterbox, you made it seem like someone hurt you. It was Jack, wasn't it?"

She stared at the cup between her palms. "I was young and stupid. We met at one of the summer parties in Harbor. I was nothing more than a one night stand."

Her eyes lifted. "A month into the fall semester, I found out I was pregnant, so I dropped out of college, came home and tried to figure out how to patch together a life."

"He didn't acknowledge –"

"No. Nothing. There was nothing I could do. I was just a local, half Odawa girl from up Middle Village. A long way from Harbor Springs."

"What happened to the baby?" Heather asked.

"I raised him," she recovered proudly. "Benjamin is his name. He's married and lives outside of Mackinac. He's made a good life."

Rick leaned back and looked meaningfully at Heather.

"I know this looks bad," Bethany repeated, "especially after I confronted him at the regatta dinner."

"You what?" Heather blurted. "What do you mean confronted?"

"I'd heard about Jack through the years in the local news for his races or through his family's philanthropy."

"You never contacted him. You had rights for God's sake," Heather said.

Bethany shook her head. "The regatta dinner was the first time I'd come in contact with him face to face in all those years."

At that moment, Jan arrived carrying a tray in one hand with two cups of coffee and holding a carafe in the other. "Sorry it took me so long." She put the full cups on the table and tilted the carafe to refill Bethany's. "What's with the meeting?" she asked innocently. "I just mentioned the Good Earth to Erasmus a couple weeks ago, and now I find you all conspiring over here in the corner." She examined their faces and found only tension. "Tell you what, I'll check back with you after a while. Rick, come get me if you need anything."

He reached over and grabbed her arm as she began to leave. "Thanks, Jan," he said simply. "I appreciate it."

"I know you do," she said with a mixture of sarcasm and warmth. "You know where to find me."

Heather waited until she was out of range. "You were saying about a confrontation."

"I know I shouldn't have, but I couldn't help it. They'd just finished introducing the caterers to the crowd, and I saw him at the table, sitting there enjoying himself. I walked over and faced him and told him I could have used his support all those years."

"Was he alone?"

Bethany shook her head. "His wife was next to him. At least, I assume it was –"

"Dark, straight hair?" Rick interrupted.

She nodded. "I kept my voice low, but I know she heard me. I was only there a moment or so."

Rick looked again at Heather, trying to decide what to do. Her shoulders lifted slightly as she barely tilted her head. "You had the motive and the means," she said softly, turning her eyes back toward Bethany, "but I do believe you."

"So do I," Rick said, "but you have to contact the police with what you know. Officer Bennett may already have found out about you. She planned to conduct additional interviews this morning. Did others at the table hear you?"

"I don't think so."

"But clearly Veronica did. Did she recognize you?"

Bethany pretended not to hear the question and leaned over to grab her purse from the empty chair next to hers. She carefully removed a folded piece of paper and placed it on the table in front of her. "You would think she should have recognized me," she said simply as she unfolded the sheet and laid if flat, rotating it so the printed list was facing them.

Rick leaned in, squinting. "Damn it," he muttered.

"Let me," Heather said grabbing his shoulder and pulling him back toward his chair. She reached across and lifted the page for a closer look. The top line was a date, followed by the words, 'Outfitter Talk – Harbor Springs' and a list of fifteen printed names and email addresses beneath. Heather glanced up. "What's this?"

"When I do local talks, I like to have guests sign in, so I can send them follow-up information later on. It's a targeted way for me to promote a community interest in foraging and, admittedly, a convenient way for me to send advertisements for my restaurant."

"You gave this talk a couple of weeks ago." Heather stated, glancing down the list of names. She paused midway and leaned in more closely, jerking her head upward suddenly. "Is this correct?"

"What'd you find?" Rick said anxiously, fumbling for his glasses.

"Now you understand," Bethany said.

Midway down the list, written in clear script was the name Veronica Cabbott. Heather sat up and glanced back and forth between them. "No, I don't understand."

Bethany rotated the page and placed her finger directly over the written name. "The woman seated next to Jack Stinson the other night, his wife – I am confident was not among the attendees at my talk the other day."

Rick leaned in. "You're certain?"

"Yes." She tapped her finger on the page. "When I heard her name this morning on the news, I remembered seeing it on the list."

"You're saying someone attended your talk and put down Veronica Cabbott's name?"

"That's the only explanation I have. And I'm certain the real Veronica Cabbott wasn't there."

"Was your talk like the one you gave at the Camp?" Rick asked.

"Mostly. I emphasized more of the culinary uses for foraged items and spent less time on the pharmacological stuff."

"What about poisonous plants?" Heather said.

"Yes."

"Hemlock?"

Bethany's expression darkened. "I talked about eradication programs for wild poisonous plants. Mostly the efforts by local agriculture to rid poisonous plants from livestock pasture land." She looked helplessly first at Heather and then to Rick. "I used a slide that shows a before and after distribution for Emmet County, mostly to emphasize how native plants are being systematically eliminated."

"Let me guess," Heather whispered.

"The slide shows the Pokeweed and Jimsonweed control projects several years ago in the area bounded by Van Road to the north and Brutus Road to the South."

"So what's the –"

"There's a link on the slide for more information about other control projects – Snakeroot, Nightshade, Lupine, Milkweed, and Hemlock."

"Do these give locations?" Rick asked.

Bethany nodded. "With enough detail to know where to go find them."

Rick leaned back and looked down at his cup of coffee, suddenly realizing he hadn't touched it. "You need to talk with Abigail."

"When?" Bethany said.

"She's in Harbor all day. I'll call her as soon as we're finished here and see if she's available first thing tomorrow? It may be easier if you meet half way. Could you come to the Camp?"

Heather put her hand on his forearm. "I've got my lab in the morning."

Rick looked at them both. "I'll confirm midday."

Bethany lifted the piece of paper and folded it back into a small rectangle. "Midday tomorrow, unless you tell me otherwise."

Chapter 12

    Heather handed each student a piece of paper and returned to the front. "Take a couple minutes to examine the information on this sheet. I consolidated your raw data for both the East Point and Grapevine feeding platforms. The tables show the percent of the dough worms taken by color for each of the eight days you collected. The first column is the yellow worms, followed by red, blue, green mimic and then green model. I kept the morning and evening data separate to see if there were differences between the percent of prey taken by time of day."

    The red haired boy raised his hand. "Go ahead, Thomas," she encouraged.

    "Are the green mimic numbers when we used arrays with more of the normal tasting green worms compared to the bad ones?"

    Heather nodded. "That's correct. For those of you who created the arrays we used each day, I suspect this makes sense. For the rest," she made eye contact with several students seated randomly about the lab, "who did data collection, this may need a little clarification." She lifted her copy from the table near where she stood. "Remember, we decided only to vary the ratio of tasty to bitter with the green worms. Some of the arrays your classmates created used twice as many green mimics as there were bitter green models. This data is given under column four. Other arrays used the opposite. This allows us a way to distinguish what effect there may be when the number of mimics exceeds the number of models. Make sense?"

"So, the birds are able to distinguish color!" said Melanie.

Heather waited to see if anyone else wanted to comment. "They certainly devoured the yellow worms," laughed another boy near the back.

"It would seem so," Heather said. "Yellow was taken at high percentages for each location no matter what day and time. Any hypotheses?"

"They like yellow?" Thomas said. This elicited several chuckles. "No, seriously. I mean, they're not quite yellow, but so many of the green caterpillars and tent worms in the trees are almost a yellowy color. Maybe the birds think the yellow dough worms are close enough."

"Which is possibly why there were some slight differences between Grapevine and East," Melanie added.

"Go on," Heather said.

"Well, there were more yellows taken from Grapevine compared to East, and this makes sense if what Thomas said was true."

"Because?" Heather encouraged.

"Because there are more deciduous trees near the Grapevine sight, which is where the tent caterpillars are."

Once again, Heather nodded her approval. "Nicely done, both of you. What about the rest? What do you make of the green data?"

"The mm ... mm ... mim ..." the boy with the stutter began. Heather waited patiently as he stopped, took a deep breath and tried again. "The mm ... mimics woo ... work when their n ... numbers are low."

Heather nodded her approval. "Good. Low

numbers of mimics do appear advantageous. I'll want you all to run some basic statistics on the data to see if it's significant, but it looks like the birds do avoid the good tasting mimics when their ratio is low. What about the model data?"

A blonde stout boy on the far side raised his hand. "So, when the number of good tasting green worms too high compared to the bad tasting ones, the birds don't discriminate any more. The total number of green worms eaten is higher than when the ratio is low."

"Again, nicely done," Heather said. "It'll be interesting to see what other differences there may be between the morning and afternoon data sets." She reached for another stack of papers on the table and handed one to each student. "This gives an overview of how to set up a basic Chi-squared test to see if any two numbers are statistically different. You'll see some of the assumptions that underlie the test given at the top. I'd like you each to work with a partner to select a comparative set of data and do some statistical testing using the Chi-squared approach, if you think it's warranted."

She then turned to the board and began writing. "Before you get started, I want to give you a heads up on a special lab I'd like to run two evenings from now." The students looked at one another, slightly surprised. Heather had written two words, *Photinus* and *Photuris* in large script. "Several of you may know my colleague Professor David Karault, who specialized in climate change on herbivore and plant dynamics. For those who haven't met him, you've probably seen him out working in the large research field above campus, the one with the big carbon dioxide tents."

"Yeah, and he's wicked good at volleyball," Thomas said smiling.

"Heather laughed. "Yes, he is." She gestured to the words on the board. "Sometimes, we get lucky, and this is one of those summers. I asked him the other day if he's seen these along the edge of the field when he's been up there in the evening."

"Well who hasn't seen a *Photinus* walking around the camp!" joked Melanie. This made everyone giggle.

"Fair enough," Heather added. "Actually, these are two genera of fireflies that we sometimes have here in northern Michigan. Normally, they'd be around the last part of June, but with the cool start to summer, they've delayed their appearance until now. You're most likely to see them on the edge of large fields near the border trees. I don't think I've ever seen them down within the Camp, at least not in the three years I've worked here."

"So, you want us to go catch fireflies?" asked an Asian boy who seldom spoke.

"Yes, in a manner of speaking. If things go as I hope, we'll go visit the upper field at dusk a couple nights from now. You're going to use video recorders to capture the signal patterns of the fireflies as they call to one another, and I'm going to have you create special maps of the timing and location of their flash patterns."

Again, the students looked at one another, slightly dumbfounded.

Heather smiled. "Ok, I can see by your faces the big question is why? Because, there is a unique and I'll admit a little nerdy mimicry relationship we might be able to record if the data collection goes well. Both genera should be out at the same time, and you might think that fireflies just flash willy nilly all over the field, but I assure you it's not so simple. The two genera have unique flash patterns, and even the males and females within a genus flash a special code to one another to attract attention. Males flash a certain way, and the females respond differently in a recognizable pattern so the male knows where to go. Now, here's where it gets interesting. The female of the *Photuris* genus is often called the femme fatale of the lightning bug world. What she does is nothing short of amazing, and what's more, etymologists have determined why she does it."

"The female *Photuris* firefly mimics the signal response pattern of the completely different species, the female *Photinus*. In doing this, she fools the male into thinking she is his potential suitor. He responds, and she continues the mimic, until they finally meet one another, either in the open field or just near the ground. The femme fatale then kills the *Photinus* male and consumes much of his organic material. She does this to gain both nutrients and, more unbelievably, she takes in a certain steroid molecule that can only be produced the by *Photinus* fireflies and not by her species. This steroid makes her unpalatable to certain predatory spiders, which in a round about way is like our mimic dough worms passing themselves off as look alikes to the bitter ones."

Thomas glanced about at his classmates, who were obviously as taken in with Heather's description as himself. "And we get to measure this?" he said, his voice clearly showing his enthusiasm.

"Hopefully," Heather replied, "We can easily research the flash patterns during our next session, get the cameras ready, and cross our fingers the weather will cooperate and the fireflies will make their appearance."

"I'm sorry," Melanie added, "That's got to be the coolest thing I've heard in a while."

Heather beamed, buoyed by their interest. "Yeah, me too, and I'm not really a bug nerd!"

#

Abigail checked her watch. "You sure you told her noon?"

Rick repositioned himself on the bench and removed his phone from his front pocket. "Positive. We've still got ten minutes." Some movement caught his attention, and he looked up toward the gravel drive, where Heather approached from the direction of the main Camp. "Here comes Heather."

They both waited until she reached the porch and joined them on the deck. "Did you tell her?"

Abigail's eyes narrowed. "Tell me what?"

Rick gave Heather a pleading expression and then turned to Abigail, "There's more to Bethany than just her expertise in poisonous plants."

"Beyond the fact she was at the regatta dinner?"

Rick's face registered surprise, "You knew?"

"Only yesterday. Her name appeared on a list I received about the wait staff and caterers. The name Poneshing kind of sticks out. I assume she's Odawa? That's an old name from out near the coast."

Rick nodded, "She was also connected to Jack Stinson."

Abigail's face drained. "That, I didn't know."

He spent the next several minutes telling her about their original meeting with Bethany, how she agreed to give a talk at the Bug Camp two weeks ago, and how she revealed to them yesterday the nature of her history with Jack Stinson. Abigail listened patiently, occasionally glancing to Heather for confirmation and interrupting only twice with questions. When he finished, she placed her right palm on her temple and rubbed slowly. "She could be lying."

"We know," Rick said. "But if that were the case, why go to the risk of telling us in the first place? Yes, we would eventually have made the inference about the hemlock and her specialty, but it's less certain the former relationship with Jack would ever be known."

Abigail appeared slightly annoyed. "Veronica Cabbott certainly didn't mention anything about an interaction with Ms. Poneshing," which would make sense if —"

"Hold on," Rick said, "Yesterday, you told me Veronica's lover was at the dinner. Since Veronica didn't mention anything about —"

"Who are you both talking about?" Heather blurted excitedly.

Rick shook his head.

Abigail pursed her lips, weighing the pros and cons. "Oh, what the hell," she sighed. "I interviewed her yesterday. She's one of the rival skippers from Harbor Springs. Evidently, she and Mr. Stinson have known each other since they were young."

Rick's face blanched. "It can't be," he stammered.

"What?" Heather looked back and forth between them.

"She didn't hide the fact she was having an affair with him."

"Who?" Heather asked again.

"Was, as in it ended some time ago, or as in still having a relationship?" Rick pressed.

"Still," Abigail replied.

Heather's voice rose an octave. "For the last time, who?"

Rick's gaze lowered, and he stared absently at the worn deck boards. "Her name is Ellen Kinnear."

"And how do you —"

He eyes lifted. "She was a part of the old group when we were kids. Jack, Ellen, John, Andrew, Peach. She lived out somewhere near Harbor and would come over to crew for some of the Wednesday and Saturday races." Rick turned to Abigail. "What else?"

"She indicated Stinson was planning to leave his wife *and* that his wife had fits of jealousy."

"Which would be an easy way of pointing suspicion at Veronica Cabbott," Rick said. "Maybe she shouldn't be ruled out as a suspect. Maybe Veronica *was* at Bethany's talk –"

Heather interrupted, "And signed her name? It's tough to believe she'd be so foolish. Plus, isn't she relatively well known in Harbor? It's too likely someone else at the talk would have recognized her."

"Unless she was disguised," Rick speculated.

Abigail shook her head. "Seems like a stretch."

Heather suddenly drew her palm upward to cover her mouth. She looked at Rick with wide eyes.

"What is it?" he said.

"A femme fatale," she said. "It's possible. We were just talking about this earlier in lab."

Abigail's voice hardened. "You were talking about the Stinson murder with your students?"

Heather ignored the reproach. She lowered her hand and reached over to grasp his wrist. "She's a mimic, using Veronica Cabbott's name as a ruse to implicate her while all the while planning to kill him."

Rick heard the sound of gravel dislodge beneath the tires of Bethany's truck as she pulled into an empty spot near the forest edge. "Yeah, it's possible. At least, it's worth a shot."

"Do you have any old photos of her?" Heather asked.

Abigail remained silent.

Rick stood and walked toward the sliding back door as Bethany approached. He glanced upward at the still trees overhead. "I just might."

"Just might what?" Bethany said as she ascended the stairs and stuck a hand out in Abigail's direction.

"Just might get a internet signal today. Give me a few minutes. I want to see if I can get a current photo."

Abigail rose and grasped the woman's hand. "Abigail Bennett. You must be Bethany Poneshing."

#

The photo was taken from another boat following closely alongside the *Dependent,* sailing in a reach somewhere out in Little Traverse Bay. Plainly visible was a three quarter view of Ellen Kinnear's face as she stood upright in the cockpit, her hand resting on the tiller extension and her eyes cast upward toward the bow. A caption beneath the photo described windy conditions on Lake Michigan for the Saturday series and mentioned Ellen's name. Bethany studied it closely for several seconds and finally returned the page to Rick.

"How certain are you?" Rick asked.

She closed her eyes and tried to imagine the audience. "There were a little over a dozen people at the talk. Most were women. She came in and sat near the back. Light blue blouse. White capris pants." Bethany opened her eyes and pointed to the photo still in his hand. "She had on a blue baseball cap with her hair tucked back in a ponytail."

Rick looked at Abigail. "What do you think?"

"I think it's thin."

"What about –"

Abigail held up her hand. "I need to meet with

her again, and it's critical I do as soon as possible, particularly with this new information. I can have a handwriting analysis done on Ms. Poneshing's list, but I'll need a sample from Ms. Kinnear for comparison. It's possible I could figure out a way to get something, but even *if* I do *and* the results are conclusive, it's still thin."

"It would prove she attended Bethany's talk and forged Veronica's name," Heather said.

"And nothing more," Abigail added.

"Why can't you just confront her?" asked Bethany.

Abigail shook her head. "Again, there's protocol. Right now, Ms. Kinnear is not an official suspect." She noticed Heather about to open her mouth. "I have to be very careful during this interview stage, even if there's reasonable cause for suspicion. At minimum, I need to get her first hand testimony and see how it matches what we already know."

Rick waved the photo. "We *already* know she falsely implicated someone."

"Careful, Rick," Abigail said. "We have to go through the proper steps. Once I have a chance to talk to her, if there's enough evidence to warrant making her an official suspect, then we'll do so. Until then, what we have is mostly circumstantial."

Rick turned to Bethany, "Do you know specifically where to find poison hemlock?"

"Yes. There are three locations with easy access close enough to Harbor Springs."

Rick saw Abigail about to protest. "Just here me out. Would these have shown up on the map link you told us about before?"

"Yes," Bethany said.

"And you're certain there's still hemlock growing there?"

"I know for a fact two of the locations have hemlock. I foraged nearby only a month ago or so."

Rick looked at Abigail. "What if Ellen was seen gathering the plants?"

"Not likely with one of the locations," Bethany said. "It's fairly far back from a two track that leads off Robinson Road. The other is in a low lying field not far from where the North Country Trail cuts through Sturgeon."

Heather shook her head. "There'd be no way to track down someone if even she was seen at either place. The dune trail into sturgeon is pretty remote."

"I think it's worth a look anyway," Rick said.

Abigail was clearly frustrated as she enunciated each word. "You need to let me conduct the investigation. I'll head over to Harbor right now and see if I can locate Ms. Kinnear."

Rick shrugged as if trying to change the subject. "There's nothing wrong with going on a little hike while we wait."

"Rick, I'm not asking."

He was about to reply when he felt Heather reach over and place her hand on top of his, giving a slight warning squeeze. "We understand," she said. "You'll let us know?"

Abigail nodded and then stood, turning to Bethany, "If I need to get in touch with you?"

"I'll be out in Good Hart, either at my home or at the restaurant."

"And you two," Abigail said glancing at Heather and then letting her eyes settle meaningfully on Rick. "I know the coverage is bad here, but I'll try your cell first."

"There's always Peg," Rick suggested.

Abigail walked over to the steps. "Be patient." She descended and began walking across the gravel drive toward the parking area a hundred yards through the trees.

Chapter 13

"It's just before that sharp curve up ahead." Heather pointed through the windshield where the road turned north and vanished into the woods.

The narrow two lane road brought them west from the small village of Bliss up onto the glacial escarpment before dropping down in a series of twisting curves until it neared the sand dunes of the Lake Michigan shoreline a hundred yards ahead through the trees. Rick slowed the car and looked for a safe place on the shoulder to pull over. A small wooden signpost came into view on the right, set back within a sandy berm at the entrance to a narrow single track trail that vanished into a thin grove of cedar and hemlock. Rick pulled over and turned off the engine.

Bethany looked around. "You brought your students here the other day?"

Heather unbuckled her seat belt and began to open the passenger door. "Last session. This dune area is one of the most well known natural representations of forest succession, so we hiked from west from the climax woods through the transitions into the dune." She stepped out and waited by the sign until the pair joined her.

"How far in?" Rick asked, glancing up toward where the trail cut into the forest.

"About a quarter mile," Bethany replied leading the way. The path undulated sharply in a series of small steep hills and valleys through a mixed forest of conifers and hardwoods, occasionally turning westward into sandy stretches where the dunes from Lake Michigan crept inward. After a while, the trail turned northeast and descended into lowland area, bordered on the far side by a boggy fen. Bethany brought them to a halt and pointed across the clearing to where the trail skirted the western edge of the water before entering once again into the trees beyond. "Over there," she said simply, stepping aside to let Rick take the lead as they approached a cluster of tall grasses dotted here and there with Black-eyed Susan, Queen Anne's Lace and Knapweed.

"Where?" Heather turned, looking among the flowers on the left side of the trail.

Bethany touched her arm and pointed to the other side, where the land descended slightly into the wet. Hidden within the tall grass rose several plants Heather initially thought was yarrow or parsnip. Their thick green stems were speckled with purple splotches, ending upward in clusters of spreading white flowers. She bent close and inspected one, cautiously reaching a hand toward one of the deep green leaves. "Safe?"

Bethany nodded. "As long as you don't crush it and put your fingers in your mouth."

Rick pulled a leaf and rolled it between his fingers. "It smells terrible." He then lifted his head and scanned the immediate area. "They're only around here?"

Bethany drew her hand in an arc that encompassed roughly several hundred square feet around where they stood. "This is the area that shows up on the state link. My guess is a few dozen groupings at most."

He looked down where the stalks disappeared

among the other grasses into the moist ground, realizing suddenly the imprint his own foot had made as he crushed the foliage in the soft earth. "Stop!"

Heather jerked upward. "What's the matter?"

He pointed to an area a few yards away. "Over there. Someone's walked through here not too long ago. You see?" Heather retraced her steps and came closer. There, among a small group of mature plants, it looked as though someone had intentionally removed something from the ground beneath.

"Oh my God," Heather whispered.

Bethany joined them and inspected the ground below. "The ground's too soft to leave any - "

Rick looked at her. "Footprint, I know." He reached into his pants pocket and removed a small ziplock bag and offered it to her. "This may be the best we can hope for. Hold this open for me, will you?" He reached over and grabbed the stalk of the plant nearest where the earth had been disturbed, using his free hand to tear away several small branches with their leaves and flowers still attached. He placed them all into the bag and retrieved it from her.

"I don't understand," Bethany said.

"It's a long shot," he replied, "but we've got the frozen sample from the gastric contents. We could have sequencing done on those samples and on this plant here to see if there's a match, assuming hemlock grows in clones." He retraced his steps through the tall grass onto the trail and closed the bag, placing it securely into his pocket. "And if any of the plant that was used to kill Jack still exists, we could try to do a match."

"I think Abigail would call that possibility a thin one," Heather said soberly, stepping past him and leading the way back down the trail toward the dunes.

"Abigail would say other things if she knew we

were here right now." Rick muttered as he followed
behind.

#

The road emerged from the trees and descended
into open farmland as they approached Bliss. Rick's cell
suddenly began to chime. Heather glanced down and
looked at his screen, barely visible inside the cup holder
between the seats. "Abigail called three times over an
hour ago." She looked up sharply. "There's a voice mail."

He nodded. "Put it on speaker."

Heather lifted the receiver and pushed the
playback button.

*"Rick, this is Abigail. I've been trying to get in
touch with you for the past hour. Call me as soon as you
get this message."*

He slowed at the intersection marking Bliss and
pulled the car over in the shoulder. "I imagine she's
wondering where the hell we've been." He dialed and
waited. "Abby, it's me."

Heather heard the tinny voice through the
receiver and saw the color drain slowly from his face. "I
understand," he said softly. A minute passed during
which he listened intently and said nothing. "When?"
His voice strained. "Yes, we'll be ready." He hung up the
phone and stared absently out the windshield, finally
turning slowly toward her with a haunted expression.
"Abigail went to Ellen's home to try and find her." He
shook his head slowly. "She's dead. Abby said she peered
through a front window and saw her body on the hallway
floor."

Bethany inhaled sharply from the back seat.

Heather was speechless for several seconds. "Did
she say how?" she whispered.

"There were several plants on the counter near the sink. Abigail said it looks like a possible suicide." His voice became detached. "The autopsy will take place quickly. We should have samples the day after tomorrow. She needs us to go ahead as we did before with Jack."

Tears formed in Heather's eyes, concern mirrored on her face. "Oh, Rick, I'm so sorry."

Chapter 14

"Where have you been?" Peg stood with her hand on the gate and watched him approach.

"Just clearing my head." He noticed her flushed cheeks. "Have you been out exercising?"

"Hell no! I was looking for you!" she lifted her arm and showed him a piece of paper held firmly between her fingers. "A letter came."

"You mean to tell me you tracked me all the way out –"

"It's from Harbor Springs," Peg interrupted.

A pained expression formed on his face. "From whom?"

Peg shook her head. "No name. Only a return address."

"Pike Road?"

She glanced down. "Yes, Pike."

Rick exhaled and walked around the gate. "I'm afraid to take a look. It's been two weeks, and I still feel-"

"I know." She lifted her hand. "Take it."

He removed the letter and held it up to examine. "What the hell could this –"

Peg had already begun walking away. "You know where to find me Erasmus, if you need me."

He looked up with a wan smile. "Thanks, Margaret." Rick opened the envelope and removed the single page, letting his eyes scan the first few lines.

Dear Rick,

I don't know exactly why, but I want you to know I loved Jack all those years. I love him still. I had hoped to rid him of her – to give him freedom from the life he chose, but something went terribly wrong, and now he's gone. Forgive me Rick for what I've done, and remember us better than we deserve.

#

Heather stepped onto the porch and walked carefully across the old boards, mindful of the places where the nails had worked their way upward. She lowered herself into the empty deck chair beside him and lifted the bottle. "Refill?"

Rick emptied the last of his red wine and held out his glass. "Thanks."

Overhead, twilight had finally given way to the coming night, and one by one the stars began to reveal themselves against the black sky through the dark boughs above. In the stillness, sound easily carried across the water, and they listened to the mixture of camp voices and the trill of summer insects.

"What did she say about the letter?" Heather asked.

"Same thing I think. She'd found enough evidence that Jack had been financially supporting Ellen for many years. My guess is Veronica Cabbott probably was aware of much, if not most, of what was going on and finally gave him an ultimatum."

"So why would Ellen put Veronica's name on the

list if she intended to get rid of her all along?"

Rick shrugged. "A twist? Maybe she thought it would look like suicide. Veronica attends Bethany's talk and is later found dead by linked poison. Who knows?" He brought the glass to his lips and took a slow sip. "Something must have gone wrong. Maybe someone accidentally switched chairs. Veronica had evidently left the table for a long period. I suppose anything's possible." He inhaled deeply. "Someone's got a camp fire."

"Peg said a group on the upper row are doing a late night vigil to watch for the raccoons."

He turned to her. "Harold never took care of that problem?"

"Oh, he did alright. The pair just came back and went underneath another cabin close by."

"You know what bothers me most?"

Heather misunderstood. "It's tough to control raccoons?"

He shook his head. "What? No, about Jack."

"Oh," she said softly. "What?"

"It was at least a couple days after his death before she ate the hemlock."

Heather nodded. "I know. I didn't want to mention it."

"And she even had talked once with Abigail, for goodness sake." He took another drink. "What the hell was she thinking?"

Heather reached over and touched his cheek. "We'll never know."

Chapter 15

"Almost there." Heather maneuvered the car on the two-track into the woods, passing through a low boggy section filled with an understory of emerald ferns.

"The only person out here is Peach."

"And her boys. William's here too."

"So you've spoken to her."

Heather laughed. "Of course, silly. She's expecting us."

Rick glanced over. "What do you have up your sleeve?"

"You'll see soon enough." The dirt road ascended slightly onto drier land and emerged from the forest into an open space where two old cottages sat next to one another on a point overlooking the lake expanse in the distance. Heather brought the car to a stop in a small parking area next to the house.

A screen door opened, and a woman stepped out to greet them. She approached Heather and gave her a warm embrace then turned to Rick with the same. "Does he know?" Her southern accent sounded mischievous.

"Know what?"

Peach laughed. "You've got a keeper here, Rick. You best marry this woman quickly, before she figures you out."

"I can't thank you enough for all your help," Heather said, looking at Rick with a hopeful expression. "I know the past few weeks were hard for you, in ways I guess only the two of you could really understand."

Peach nodded and her expression softened. "You ready?"

"Ready for what!" he nearly shouted. "I don't know what you two have schemed, but you might as well –" He paused, seeing tears in the corners of Heather's eyes.

She took his hand and led him around the cottage until they came to where the dock thrust outward from the shore. Rick stopped suddenly as his eyes found the boat moored a dozen yards off the end. Her hull was an aged cream color with a black mast that shot upward twenty-six feet into the air. She was rigged with a worn mainsail and jib, the former bearing a faded red lightning bolt insignia in its upper third. Both sails flapped idly in the offshore breeze, causing the painter line to pull back and forth slightly against the mooring like a dog tugging at a leash wanting to go.

He stood silently for nearly a minute, letting his eyes admire her beautiful lines. "I didn't think there were any left."

Heather squeezed his hand. "Peach said she knew there was one in storage down the shore."

"That's Graham's old boat, isn't it?"

Peach nodded. "Dana said it'd be ok with him to drop her in and rig her. You've got Heather here to thank for it."

"Only for the idea," Heather said. "Peach and Dana rigged it for you."

Rick turned to them both, tears now in his eyes. "We can go?"

"You told me you'd take me sailing some day. Why not today?"

Peach smiled at him and started to back away toward the cottage. "Imagine that. Erasmus Parsons speechless. That's worth the price of admission." She laughed then. "I expect you know what you're doing out there Rick. Why don't you two go have a little fun." She looked again at the boat and the let her eyes scan the water beyond, seeing the chop out past the point where the breeze built over the trees above.

#

Rick drew the tiller nearer, bringing the bow off the wind toward the direction of Fishtail in the distance. "Ease the jib, will you?"

Heather had quickly learned that meant the same thing as *let it out*. She felt the boat heel slightly to leeward as they arced around, and she lowered herself down into the cockpit. "Does it feel the same?"

He laughed. "Yes and no. It'd be better if I was eight inches shorter and scrambling up on the foredeck like the petrified boy I used to be."

She turned her head from one side to the other, scanning the horizons. "I think we're the only ones out here."

He motioned across the starboard bow. "Pontoon boat way over there. Probably one of ours."

The breeze had died slightly as they sailed past Bentley point on their port side. Rick waved at someone high on the bluff in front of the Mayfield house. He listened to the sound of the waves slapping gently against the hull and closed his eyes to feel the summer wind across the water. After a moment, he opened them and found her looking at him.

"You ok?"

"Like I said, yes and no." He smiled almost plaintively and moved his outstretched arm like a second hand sweeping the shoreline. "Graham, Bud, Maury,

164

Doc, Earl, John." He then turned and gestured loosely behind him in the direction of the other bay. "Jack and Tom." He met her eyes again. "In many ways, they were a big part of my growing up here." He gripped the tiller more firmly. "These boats, the people. It makes me sad they're all gone."

Heather sat patiently, letting his words unfold.

"Look out across the water." He waited while she scanned the horizon. "It looks almost the same as it did all those years ago. It feels almost the same." He then held his hand up to show her. "But this isn't the same. I'm not the same. And now, with Jack and Ellen gone. I just feel –"

"You should feel lucky to have been a part of all that," she said hopefully. "And not all of the Lightnings are gone, it would seem. There may still be one or two hidden away, waiting for someone to take them out again."

He pulled the tiller closer and ducked slightly, reaching up to grab the boom as it came slowly across in a jibe.

"We're not heading back yet, are we?"

"Not quite," he said hopefully. "Just a new course. Let's keep going awhile longer. It's too beautiful to go back just yet."

Author's Notes:

As with the first two books about Erasmus Parsons and the Bug Camp, I know I've greatly oversimplified the daily academic life at the University of Michigan Biological Station. I so admire the history of that institution and the nature of the teaching and research they conduct. Do yourself a favor and go walk the trails along East Point or through the woods within Grapevine. Say hello to the students and faculty who roam the campus. Trust me, you'll feel welcome.

Of course, I've also taken a few liberties with the jurisdiction of my fictional character Abigail Bennett. Though she is based out of Cheboygan, for the sake of the story I conveniently let her conduct her investigation in Harbor Springs.

In the chapter when Heather and Rick meet one of the Bug Camp students along the Grapevine Trail, the student mentions she's reading a book by one of my favorite authors – Virginia Eifert. No other book reminds me more of being at Douglas Lake than her wonderful Land of the Snowshoe Hare.

For a few summers, when I was between thirteen and fifteen, I crewed for Mr. and Mrs. Osgood on their Lightning. They, like so many of the summer residents along the shore, became members of my adolescent extended family, and I am grateful for their friendship those many years ago.

The days of Lightnings have long gone, and this is a shame. For at least a dozen years, nearly every summer Saturday was occupied with these magnificent boats, and it was such a sight to see their brilliant white sails and colorful spinnakers racing about one bay or another. I feel so blessed to have the memories of these days.

Following the race, and after we'd dissemble the rigging and stow the sails, I'd be invited in for a cup of water or milk and a few of Aunt Thilda's cookies. They were unique, partly because I was told they were Mr. Osgood's (Bud's) favorite:

Cream together the following:
- 1 Stick Oleo
- ½ Cup Lard
- 1 $7/8$ Cup Sugar

2 Eggs – Add to the above and mix well

Add to the above and mix well:
- 1 Cup Buttermilk
- 1 tsp. vanilla

Mix the following well with the above:
- 1 tsp. nutmeg
- ½ tsp. salt
- 1 tsp. soda
- 4 cups of unbleached flour

Refrigerate the mixture at least 2 hours.

Drop by soupspoon onto greased cookie sheet. Dip a flat-bottomed glass in sugar and lightly flatten cookies.

Bake 12 minutes until lightly golden at 350 degrees.

Optional – sprinkle over with sugar

Made in the USA
Middletown, DE
04 November 2020